"Stop fighting what you feel."

Ryan took a step closer. "You know we've been headed for this moment from the beginning."

Sunny didn't—couldn't—stop him as he covered her mouth with his own, slipping his tongue inside, caressing her inner warmth in rhythm to the pounding of her heart. Then his fingers moved to the tightly drawn sash at her waist, loosening it and letting her robe fall open. He reached in and touched her breast, skimming it lightly, starting a thousand fires just beneath the skin, fires that ran down every pulsing vein in her body and settled between her legs.

Ryan didn't try to hide his arousal as he pulled her hard against him. "I have to make love to you, Sunny. We both have to know if this is just a fantasy or if it's real."

Her knees trembled, her pulse raced. This was the moment of truth. Then, almost of their own volition, her fingers tugged down on his briefs. She looked at him and caught her breath.

"You said your bed or mine," she whispered. "Looks like it's going to be mine."

Dear Reader,

Joining the grand roster of Temptation authors is unbelievably exciting. And being asked to write the first book in the Sweet Talkin' Guys miniseries was a particular thrill and a challenge. After all, it's not easy creating a hero who personifies every woman's secret fantasy.

I hope that this will be the beginning of a new and very personal relationship between you and me. So let me tempt you with my first to-die-for Temptation hero, Lord Sin. He's an enigmatic, internationally famous exotic dancer, who's determined to keep his true identity a secret—until he runs into a bright-eyed, idealistic young reporter who's determined to *expose* him to the world. Lies meet the truth, sunshine meets shadows and the unmasking begins.

I try to put a lot of humor, joy and love in all my stories. After all, I come from the land of moonlight and magnolias where true love, hot sex and happily ever afters are very real to me. When you're finished reading *Baring It All,* take a cold shower, then let me know what you think. You can write to me at: P.O. Box 67, Smyrna, GA 30082.

Sincerely,

Sandra Chastain

Sandra Chastain
BARING IT ALL

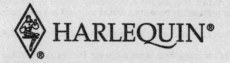

HARLEQUIN®

TORONTO • NEW YORK • LONDON
AMSTERDAM • PARIS • SYDNEY • HAMBURG
STOCKHOLM • ATHENS • TOKYO • MILAN • MADRID
PRAGUE • WARSAW • BUDAPEST • AUCKLAND

For Ann White, who always asks,
"What's he/she feeling here?"

For the over one million readers who've read my stories.
Writing is the wellspring of my life from which I draw
sustenance. You make that possible. I hope I entertain,
satisfy and bring you joy.

ISBN 0-373-25868-2

BARING IT ALL

Copyright © 2000 by Sandra Chastain.

This edition published by arrangement with Harlequin Books S.A.

® and TM are trademarks of the publisher. Trademarks indicated with
® are registered in the United States Patent and Trademark Office, the
Canadian Trade Marks Office and in other countries.

Visit us at www.romance.net

Printed in U.S.A.

1

RYAN MALONE SAW HER the minute she walked into The Palace Of Sin. She was all legs in an emerald-green gown that was split from the floor to a spot high on her hips that screamed of her lack of undergarment. Her hair was Pretty-Woman-red, falling in a wild mass of curls across her shoulders. He had a sudden mental picture of those red curls cascading across a white satin pillow. He didn't have to ask, he was already certain the color was natural. She was hot, ready to brand any man who dared to touch her.

A totally irrational jolt hit Ryan in the pit of his stomach—like nothing he'd ever felt before. He knew now what "knees going weak" meant. This kind of reaction was supposed to happen to the women in the audience, not to him. Wearing no jewelry, nothing to take a man's eye away from the woman, she was spectacular. Still, an almost imperceptible slump of her shoulders said she might not be entirely comfortable.

Although he'd quit performing five years ago, this night would be the public ending of Lord Sin's career as the most successful male stripper in history. And Ryan Malone, always in control, was suddenly awash in feelings he couldn't identify. Nostalgia? Intense desire brought on by emotion? He didn't know how to explain or control the turbulence of his physical reaction to the woman.

Normally, as Lord Sin, he would have passed on a woman like her and chosen a patron who was what he politely termed "lonely." But nothing about tonight was normal, certainly not his physical reaction to the siren in green.

The redhead walked past one of the booths selling roses, paused and gave a puzzled look at the buyers. He frowned. Any other woman would have given the baskets of roses a smile or a glance of longing. But not this one. She took a deep breath and kept going, as if she were looking for someone.

But no one came forward to join her. Maybe she was alone. He liked that idea, then wondered why. A beautiful woman alone was a Ryan Malone thought and tonight he was Lord Sin. He also wondered how she'd react to Sin's performance. Would she focus her concentration on him? Or would she be as indifferent to his dancing as she was to the roses?

He considered that and felt his lips curl into a reckless smile. Indifferent? Not if he had anything to do with it. Tonight he'd change his routine. Tonight Lord Sin would give his best performance; he'd play to her—alone. By the time the curtain came down, she'd leave The Palace Of Sin aching with desire. He certainly was.

As always, the front row of tables along the stage was vacant. His assistant, Lottie, earphone discreetly hidden in her left ear, waited below for him to decide who'd occupy them. Tonight, because the entire program had been designed as a fund-raiser, catering to the wealthy, she'd allowed for the possibility of escorts for the women, but so far, the redhead seemed to be alone.

As if she knew she was being stared at, the object of Lord Sin's attention looked around once more, then glided toward the entrance with long fluid movements that verified his earlier speculations about what she *wasn't* wearing beneath her dress. As she walked, he caught the flash of bare flesh, a warm peach color that said she liked the sun as much as he. He wondered if she looked like that all over.

A dancer or perhaps an athlete, her grace was obvious in

her walk. But who was she? Ryan Malone thought he knew every single society woman in Atlanta. The cost of the tickets tonight should mean that the attendees were all well-heeled. Only wealthy women had been invited to the Valentine Gala at the Palace this evening. She spoke briefly with a big burly man carrying a television camera who handed her a microphone. When she stepped up and began talking to a couple just entering the theater, he had his answer.

She was a member of the press. One he hadn't met. Must be new in town. He grimaced, a charged feeling rippling down his spine at the challenge. "Lottie," he spoke into the mike attached to his jacket pocket. "Put the redhead in the green dress in the center seat."

On the floor below, the elegant older woman looked up at his spot in the shadows and frowned. "The redhead may look like a society girl, boss, but she's a reporter. Lay off."

"I know. None of the reporters who tried to interview me ever looked like her. If they had, I might have been a lot more cooperative. Tonight, in honor of Lord Sin's final performance, Lottie, I'm going to give myself a treat and give *her* the royal treatment."

"What's got into you, you rascal? You've avoided the press for ten years and now you're playing to a reporter?"

"Playing. Yeah, I like that."

"Too big a risk, boss. Tonight Lord Sin retires. As Ryan Malone, you're free, just like you planned. Why take a chance on her finding out that you're really Jackson Lewis Ivy? Unless you've changed your mind and want the world to know what kind of scoundrel your late father was."

"I don't care about Jack Ivy or his father. This is Lord Sin's night. With the redhead for inspiration, my performance will be his crowning glory. Sin's been good to me and he deserves to have a little personal fun."

"Hah! Don't tell me that. Lord Sin always had fun. I don't

know why you ever quit performing. You were a master showman. You loved the stage."

"I loved the money, Lottie. I could make all those rich women feel good, take their money, and they never knew who I was."

"It was more than that. You loved to make women feel special. You loved making love with your body and with that low, sexy whisper."

"Still do, darling. I just do my lovemaking in private now."

"Take up with that redhead and your lovemaking won't be private long. She's with WTRU."

"Of course. The station known for its exposés." He laughed. "I like it. That makes it even more of a challenge for Lord Sin. In spite of that dress, I don't think she's happy about covering Lord Sin's farewell. I'm going to have to win her over."

"Sin, don't get crazy now and take a chance on ruining what you've built. You know that if anyone found out you were really Jack Ivy it could put you at risk again. That's why you gave yourself a new name. Now Sin and Jack will be gone and Ryan Malone, real estate tycoon, is above reproach." Her voice turned serious. "I think it's time for you to find a respectable woman and get married."

"Respectability," he repeated. "Respectability was always the goal, Lottie, but it wasn't mine I was concerned about." His voice went suddenly tight. "I just wanted to give my mama what she never had. She may have been a nobody, but when I'm done, all those people who turned their backs on her, including my dear daddy's family, will know and remember *her* name long after Lord Sin and Ryan Malone are distant memories."

"Your mother would have been just as proud of Lord Sin. She would have loved the man you became, no matter his profession or what name he used. Now, are you sure you want the reporter to have the seat of honor?''

He nodded and watched as Lottie moved across the lobby and spoke to the redhead. Damn! He should have asked her name. No, that was part of *her* mystery. He'd know her soon enough. But more important, she'd know Lord Sin. At least, he planned to make her want to. For now, he'd just listen.

SUNNY FELT AS IF she'd been swept away to the land of the Arabian Nights. The building, with its onion-shaped domes outside and Eastern decor inside, was a bit worn but it was still amazing. She stood in the reception area stalling while she looked around. If this was the big time, she was going to have to find a way to fit in. Covering a Valentine's Day charity fund-raiser where the prime attraction was a male stripper known as Lord Sin was a far cry from the investigative reporting she'd expected to do on her new job with WTRU TV. What was she doing here? She ought to be back in South Georgia covering the February meeting of the Kiwanis Club for the Martinsville Times.

"Well?" Walt, her cameraman, prodded. "Shall we go to work, or are we just a couple of groupies ogling the rich and famous?"

"We...we go to work." But she didn't move.

"Look, this isn't exactly my cup of tea either. I videotape sporting events, not strippers."

"And I'm an investigative reporter, not a...a voyeur," she snapped.

"Not yet, Miss Clary. So far, you're neither one and you won't ever be unless we go inside."

Sunny swallowed the lump in her throat and nodded. "Sorry, Walt. Guess I'm just a little nervous."

He gave her an amused glance. "Hum. I would have said cold."

In his Falcons' Starter jacket, Walt was as out of place in this gathering as Sunny was in the slinky dinner gown. The butterflies in her stomach reminded her that she was country casual, not a glamor girl. The joke about everyday reporters was that you could always spot them because they were the grungiest people at any function. She still didn't understand why the station had been willing to spring for a dress for *her* even if it was her first official appearance as a representative for WTRU.

Her new boss, Ted Fields, had taken a chance on hiring her after she'd been...released was the polite term...from her job as a reporter for the *Times*. Calling herself a reporter was just an exaggeration. She'd covered local events and meetings, sold ad copy and written a column called *Happenings in Martinsville,* which didn't even have her byline on it. If she'd described Candy Smithwick's wedding dress wrong, she could have understood what happened, but she still couldn't believe that her discovery of political wrongdoing had cost her job. Her editor, the man she'd thought was becoming more than just a friend, explained that the truth could hurt the county and her story would not be printed. When Sunny argued, wild rumors began to fly that her ambition had led her to speculation and exaggeration. Her credibility tumbled. In the end, she became the scapegoat and the politicians still had their jobs. Money spoke louder than words.

A flood gave her a chance to do some remote coverage for WTRU which brought her to Ted Fields's attention. The hardest thing about relocating was leaving her father behind.

Lord Sin would be her first story for WTRU. Maybe it did make some kind of sense. A reporter whose credibility was zilch ought to be just about right for covering a scandalous event where a stripper was donating a million-dollar piece of real estate formally known as *The Palace Of Sin* to the Atlanta Arts Council for a community theater.

For now she was trying to get past the tattered grandeur of that Moorish palace and get her bearings. Ted had given her a tiny tape recorder, now hidden in her purse, and a guest list for the gala affair, with a few lines of description beside each name. Even if she was new to Atlanta, she didn't need the notes to recognize two of the beautiful people, Sam and Nikki, hosts of Atlanta's top morning radio show—their billboards were everywhere. With them were the mayor and his wife and the president of one of the local colleges. As Ted had forecast, the audience was mostly women. But what surprised Sunny was the number of younger women in attendance, and something told her that charity wasn't what attracted them. She hadn't expected to get a personal interview with Lord Sin tonight, but the number two man on her interview list, Ryan Malone, the real estate tycoon who was running the show, was missing as well.

She was ready to signal for Walt to begin taping when she was intercepted by a statuesque silver-haired woman in a purple dinner gown. "With Lord Sin's compliments," she said coolly, handing Sunny a ticket. "He's arranged for you to have a seat, close to the stage."

Sunny was taken aback. "Me? Why?"

The woman in purple forced a faint smile. "Lord Sin always selects a special guest to honor."

"And he *selected* me?" She spoke with the same frosty air that Lord Sin's messenger had used. "Where is he?" She looked up, studying the private balconies hugging the stage, feeling an odd sense of being watched nudging at her. Why would he *select* her? She shifted her tiny shoulder bag higher on her shoulder and said, "I'd like to meet him."

Ignoring Sunny's request, the woman withdrew her hand.

"This seat is normally considered an honor, but if you'd pre-fer to sit elsewhere, I'm sure he'll understand."

Sunny would prefer to sit anywhere else, but Lord Sin was her focus and she was not about to blow any chance of meet-ing him. This might not be real news, but Sunny Clary al-ways did her job. When Ted Fields had told her that after ten years of unbelievable success, Lord Sin's identity was still a mystery, she knew *that* was her story—her chance to prove herself. And she had to succeed.

Her father had gotten past the lies that ruined his reputa-tion and sent him to jail for a crime he didn't commit. On his release, he'd made a new life for himself, and so could she. She'd made a vow not to rest until she'd done here in Atlanta what she'd been blocked from doing in South Georgia—re-port the truth. She just hadn't expected the truth to be about a male stripper.

"No, thank you, I'll accept his gift," she said primly, then squared her shoulders. If he'd *selected* her, he had to have seen her. Somewhere he was watching the proceedings. Maybe the green dress was worth her discomfort. He didn't know that it was rented, that it was her badge of courage. "Tell Lord Sin I'll look forward to being favored."

The woman in purple cleared her throat in resigned dis-approval. "You should also know that photographs are not permitted during his performance."

At that moment the lights flickered and summoned Lord Sin's representative and his guests into the club. Sunny sug-gested that Walt should stand against the wall out of sight and tape as much of Lord Sin's performance as possible. "Let's try to get a good close-up of his face," she added.

Clutching her seat of honor ticket, Sunny stepped inside the main room and gasped. From the streets of Cairo she'd left Egypt and entered the Sheik's palace. The stage was draped with a red velvet curtain that wasn't one of the Valentine's Day decorations. Overhead there was no ceiling, rather a night sky filled with twinkling stars. As the orchestra played "Some Enchanted Evening," Sunny took her center stage seat at a tambourine-size table only large enough for her purse and a fat cream-colored candle that twanged when she flicked it with her fingernail. It wasn't real. Somehow that seemed appropriate.

When the last strains of music died away, the curtains parted and a man holding a microphone and a rose stepped out. "Good evening, ladies and gentlemen. I'm Ryan Malone and, on behalf of the Arts Council and our benefactor, Lord Sin, I'd like to welcome you to our Valentine fund-raiser for the new Community Theater."

From the moment Ryan Malone stepped from between the folds of the curtain, Sunny's mind went into some kind of surreal overdrive. Her heart literally lurched and she could hardly breathe. The man was magnificent. In a black collarless tux with a crisp white shirt, Ryan Malone was tall and lean and dark. Ten years ago, every afternoon soap opera would have cast him as their resident bad boy. Now he might be older, more polished, with a hint of silver in his midnight-black hair, but the suggestion of danger was still there.

There was an enthusiastic outbreak of applause followed by "We hope to raise enough money tonight to turn this building into a state-of-the-art community theater. So, if you haven't already done so, stop at one of our booths on the way out and buy your sweetheart a rose." He laughed lightly and added, "Of course we'd appreciate it if you'd wrap the rose in a nice check for the Arts Council."

Ryan Malone was close enough to Sunny that she could have reached out and touched him. He never made direct eye contact with her. It was just as well. She'd have imploded, leaving nothing but the green dress in her seat.

Every molecule of her body was, for lack of a better word, shimmering. There had been men in her life before, but there had never been an earth-moving relationship. Not even close. Now she was experiencing such an acute physical reaction that she entirely missed what he was saying. Unexpectedly, he leaned down, handed her the rose he was carrying and winked, then stepped back between the curtains. The stage went black, leaving Sunny Clary stunned in the darkness. Ryan Malone knew how to get to a woman and he'd done it without saying a word.

There was a rectangle of paper wrapped around the stem of the rose that was probably a check. Great bit, Malone, she thought, letting out the breath she was holding. He was setting an example for the other guests. Apparently Lord Sin wasn't the only showman present. And if he was half as sexy as this Malone, she was beginning to get a hint of the stripper's appeal.

Next a local rock group recently nominated for a Grammy performed their hit song to tempered applause. Then the outer curtain was raised for a beautifully choreographed modern dance presentation, and, finally, an original composition by the symphony who'd donated their services as the orchestra for the evening. By the time they'd finished, Sunny had gathered her senses and given herself a stern talk about staying focused on her assignment instead of Ryan Malone. She'd turn the check over to the council and send the rose home with Walt for his wife. For now, Sunny Clary, inquiring reporter, was ready for the grand finale, the last performance of Lord Sin.

Once more the theater went dark. The orchestra began to play a haunting melody. The curtain went up, revealing the skyline of a Far Eastern city in the background. The stage had been transformed into the balcony of a palace in old Baghdad. Someone in the audience must have rubbed Aladdin's brass lamp. Stars twinkled in the distance while clouds moved across the night sky. Sunny opened her purse and flicked on the recorder and placed it on the table beside the fake candle. The melody would be good background sound for the interview. The music increased in intensity, as did the tension in the audience. Then came a crescendo of sound and a swirl of smoke and there he was.

Wearing the flowing purple and golden robes of an Arabian prince, Lord Sin sat astride a white stallion who held its head as proudly as the masked performer he was carrying. The horse stood motionless, until his master dismounted, administered an affectionate pat and let him go. A shake of his mane and the horse raced offstage and vanished into the wings. Then the smoke rose once more and Sin was alone on the balcony. Clouds seemed to surround him as he moved stealthily forward, his body swaying to the tinny sound of the flute and the heartbeat of the drums. An intense inner passion seemed to drive the dancer's fluid movement.

From the cobbled floor, Lord Sin nimbly leaped onto a wall, his golden robe billowing out, revealing a tantalizing glimpse of flesh beneath. Somehow, the music and the man gave the illusion of distance. Then, swaying and dancing nimbly along the top of the wall, he moved closer to the front of the stage.

Sunny felt herself leaning forward, shook her head and sat up straight. She didn't know what the other women were doing, but she knew that this man was a master of seduction. Finally, he reached the front of the stage that extended in the audience. The music died down and she realized that he was speaking. At first the voice was just lyrical, deep and throaty, not so much words as sounds. Finally, he looked down into the audience and, for just a moment, straight at her.

He wore a mask that covered his face and head. Only his

eyes and mouth were exposed. From beneath that mask a mass of golden curls fell across his shoulders.

"Hello, my lady in green. Welcome to Sin's house. You know about sin, don't you?" He paused and waited, as if he expected her to answer.

She swallowed hard and let out a deep breath.

"No? Then I'll consider it my pleasure to make you want to."

Someone behind Sunny whispered, "Oh, Lordy, he's looking at me. I'm going to faint right here in front of God and everybody."

The woman was wrong. Lord Sin was looking at Sunny Clary and he was talking to her. She felt every word reach inside her and snatch her breath away. There was no air. The crowd all seemed to inhale at the same time. She stared up at him, trembling, shaking with a need that came out of nowhere. The fantasy setting. The hypnotic effect of the music. Lord Sin was a David Copperfield illusion, a dream lover. The voice, a melodic whisper, indistinguishable, yet compelling, saying the kinds of things women secretly wanted to hear. All combined to weave his magic and create desire.

Sunny Clary was caught up in the spell of a master craftsman, the mysterious, passionate Lord Sin. At that moment, her rational mind knew that the story, whatever it turned out to be, was more than she'd bargained for. The sensual woman within her knew she'd never give up until she'd experienced the truth—whatever it was.

2

SUNNY GAVE HIM CREDIT, Lord Sin knew how to set a scene. There was a subtle scent of jasmine in the air, and the heated kind of stillness that would drive a passionate woman from her bed to walk on the balcony in the moonlight. The music softened to the lonely wail of a single flute. In the distance a drumbeat echoed across the night.

The low whisper of his voice began once more. "Just use your imagination, darling. Close out everything. We're alone together. Feel how I touch you." She could have sworn she felt a faint feathery sensation skitter across her breasts, as though she'd been caressed.

She gasped. How in the world could the man's voice create such feelings? It had to be some kind of hypnotism. But how could that be? Though Lord Sin's face was turned toward her, she could see neither his eyes nor his mouth. The deep fire of his voice was an illusion. Still, its very timbre fed the unmistakable arc between them. In spite of her best efforts, her breath quickened and she felt an answering throb inside her. "No," she said. "You're not getting to me."

"I want you," he whispered, as if he'd heard the words she hadn't known she'd spoken aloud. "You don't have to speak. I see the blaze in your eyes. Let yourself go. Think of how we would be—our bodies joined, our lips together."

Sin waited for a moment. Then his expression registered surprise, as if some unseen spirit had touched him. He caught his robe, ruffled it and pulled it over his face so that

he disappeared into the darkness. A collective moan rose
from the audience. But not one woman moved. Other than
the plaintive cry of the music, there was not a breath of
sound in the theater.

As mysteriously as he'd vanished, Lord Sin reappeared in
midair, atop an onion dome at the corner of the balcony. A
violin joined the flute and drum and Sin rippled his robe
once more, giving the audience a tantalizing glimpse of his
body beneath as he leaped to the floor. Then the robe was
gone and the man stood, silhouetted by the illusion of moonlight, his body nude, yet not, shimmering in the light. She
could see the muscles in his thighs and chest quiver as he
breathed. Like some jungle creature poised to ravage its
prey, he was truly magnificent.

Sensually, slowly, his fingers began to move. He reached
out, his palm touching the face of an unseen lover, lingering
there, then moving down the column of a neck and lower,
cupping the breasts of a woman who existed only in the
mind of the watcher. He bent his head and there was no
doubt that he was kissing her. With his other hand he
reached down and seemed to pull her lower body to his. You
could almost see her clasp his neck and arch her body upward. Like graceful, ghostly figures dancing through the silver smoke and golden clouds, he moved across the balcony
with this imaginary woman. Like a man enchanted, he
pulled her against him so that his lips could touch what no
one but he could see.

Sunny didn't have to be told that every woman watching
could feel his mouth on her own. His breathing, fast and
shallow, grew louder. Then, just when he seemed to have
reached the point of an explosion, Sin flung out one hand,
sprinkling the audience with particles of fiery embers that
flared, burned out, leaving only the shadow of their path in
the darkness. The stage went black.

Sin's disembodied voice remained. "Oh, yes, my lady of fire. You want me, too. You feel my lips touching yours. Tonight, you'll have erotic dreams of me and maybe I'll come to you in secret. Not on a stage in a fantasy but to your bed, at the darkest hour of the night."

A moment later he was back at center stage, on one knee, his arms extended. Imploring. His imaginary lover was gone, leaving him bereft in the artificial moonlight. He lowered his head and, almost in anguish, flung one arm across his chest. He looked as if he was nude but he was not. Instead, he wore a flesh-toned fabric that fit him like a second skin, revealing every ripple of movement.

The drumbeat grew louder. The man was on fire and so was his audience.

Sunny shifted her weight, trying to erase the responding quiver of heat building inside of her. Lord Sin stood and reached out for her. A moan and a leap took him to the top of the wall and back to a spot directly in front of Sunny. The skintight costume was so transparent that she could see the hair on his chest, the clenching of muscles in his thighs, the fullness that hinted of arousal. He was caught up in desire. If he was faking, Lord Sin was a master at his craft. He moaned, his breath turning into a gasping pant in the sudden dead silence. In search of his imaginary lover, the dancer swept about the stage, each move more desperate. The tempo of the music began to build once more. A woman across the room let out a husky gasp. Sunny shook her head in a useless attempt to regain control of her own mind and body.

Sin was moving toward her. Reaching the spot where she sat, the dancer stopped. "Don't lie to yourself, darling. Your body is reaching out to mine even if your mind denies it. You and I were meant to be one. Together we'll make a fire like you've never known. And when we love, the world will burn."

The music rose to a crescendo and the stage went dark for the final time.

For a long minute, not one person in the audience moved. Sunny sat transformed, stunned. What had happened here? How had the man taken such overwhelming control of his audience? She felt her unused notepad slide from her lap but she hadn't the strength to retrieve it. Her nerve endings were still tingling, protesting the abatement of the fire that had flamed them.

"What? How?" she finally whispered. "How did he do that?"

"I don't know," Walt's booming voice said as he crouched in the darkness beside her table. "But I wish he'd bottle the stuff. I'd take it home and spoon some into my wife's cereal."

Sunny looked at Walt. She shook her head, trying desperately to gather her senses. "Did we get him on tape?"

"No, I didn't videotape anything."

"Did they stop you?" Sunny's voice might be in outer space, but the rest of her was still in a fiery pit. The theater lights came on, softly, maintaining the mood.

"You bet. The minute I hoisted my camera onto my shoulder there was a man beside me, shaking his head. He didn't say anything but I got the message. From then on, I was just a member of the audience. Never saw anything like it. I feel like I've been barbecued. From the inside out. Me—a guy. Don't you ever tell my wife."

"He's using some kind of mass hypnosis," she said, her voice tight and low. She leaned over to retrieve her pad.

Then she heard him. "Did you like my dancing, darling?"

"What the hell?" she swore.

"Not hell, darling, heaven," Lord Sin whispered.

"A microphone," Sunny said. "You put a microphone in

the candle holder." She stared at the device on the table. "When my boss, Ted Fields, sent me over here, he said you spoke directly to the women in your audience. I didn't believe him."

"Not to all of them. Tonight, I spoke only to you."

Walt groaned. "The boss was right. The man's a hypnotist. He's got you talking to a candle. And heaven help us all, the candle's talking back."

"Shush!" Sunny said, her finger against her lips.

"Not women," Sin corrected. "Couldn't you tell? Tonight my performance was just for you."

Sunny shook her head vigorously. Maybe she was kidding herself but she had the intoxicating impression that he was still as aroused as she. Was that the secret of his success, making every woman feel as if she were totally desirable? Pulling on every ounce of her professional control, she marshaled her thoughts and switched into reporter mode. "Thank you for the special attention, Lord Sin. But if you believe you were arousing me," she added more bravely than she felt, "you're out of your mind."

"Oh?" He didn't try to conceal the amusement in his raw-silk voice. "I don't think so. I watched you. I know what I feel. Don't pretend I didn't get to you."

Sunny swallowed hard. "Well, you're wrong. I'm not easily—seduced—by a voice. You'll have to do better than that."

"Sorry, my love, that's impossible. Didn't you hear? This is Lord Sin's last performance."

"But I have it straight from your own lips." She was thinking desperately. "Lord Sin promised me that he'd make love to me soon. What's the matter? Aren't you up to seducing a real woman? Or do you just talk out of your candle?"

He laughed, his deep voice soft and hoarse. "Oh, I'm up to it, all right. I'll even admit it, you aroused me, too. It's been years since a woman has had that effect on me on stage. Why do you think I didn't strip to my G-string like I usually do?"

That thought almost did her in. "Considering the fact that whatever it was you were wearing was like wearing nothing at all, I hadn't thought about your G-string one way or the other."

"But you will, my beauty. You will. And if you really want me...I suppose we might meet again before I disappear forever. I've never indulged myself. For once, I just might."

"When?"

But the voice was gone. And she hadn't pinned him down for an interview. Her big chance and she'd failed and it was her own fault. Where had her mind been? Drowning in the physical sensation he'd created, that's where. The scoundrel was everything they'd said he was. But *who* was he?

Sunny came to her feet. "Get to the front door, Walt. If Lord Sin comes that way, video him, his car—whatever."

"Where are you going?"

"To his dressing room. Please, we have to hurry!"

"You got it," Walt said, muttering as he left. "Wish I'd brought my wife. She'll never believe what I saw."

But a quick trip to his dressing room confirmed to Sunny that it was empty. Not even his costume remained. Sunny was beginning to wonder if Lord Sin was real.

"MAY I HELP YOU?"

Sunny turned to face the same woman who'd delivered her seat of honor ticket. "I was looking for Lord Sin."

"I'm sorry, Miss..."

"Clary," Sunny said. "Sara Frances Clary. But everyone calls me Sunny."

"...Clary, but he's already left the building."

"I don't understand how I missed him, Miss...?"

"Lamour. Lottie Lamour," the gray-haired woman answered pleasantly.

"Well, I suppose I'll just have to—to make an appointment for tomorrow," Sunny said dejectedly.

"I'm very sorry but that won't be possible," Lottie said and turned to walk away.

"Just a minute," Sunny said, "you don't understand. This is my first assignment. Lord Sin donated this building to the Arts Council and I'm covering the fund-raiser for WTRU."

Lottie kept walking, drawing Sunny away from the dressing rooms. "And I'm certain you'll cover it very well."

"But surely Lord Sin would want to be given credit for this wonderful evening."

Lottie stopped and turned back to face her. "Of course, my dear. And you'll do that, won't you?"

"I need to talk with him," Sunny insisted. "Every reporter gives his subject a chance to respond."

"But Lord Sin isn't your subject," the older woman said patiently. "Your story is the theater."

"No, the theater is only window-dressing," Sunny said. "My story is the man."

Lottie's lips curved into a smile but her eyes were cold. "Good night, Miss Clary."

Sunny watched her walk away. There was no possibility she was going to reach Sin through Miss Lottie. She'd have to find another way to get to him. Sunny called after her, "Please thank Lord Sin for the seat of honor. Tell him I look forward to meeting him again."

She'd check with Walt but she already knew that he wouldn't have seen the mystery man leave the theater. There were probably secret entrances and exits that nobody but the dancer knew about. She swore again under her breath. Then, confirming the presence of her tape recorder in her purse, Sunny hurried across the stage and down the steps. With the recorder directly beside the candle she had to have captured the dancer's voice.

Dancer. She'd called him a stripper before but he was truly more than that. Showman, entertainer, magician, hypnotist. She'd totally underestimated the extent of his sorcery and the difficulty she'd faced. Even knowing what was said about the man, she'd admit it, she'd let him get to her. Well, she wasn't giving up her search, but tonight she resigned herself to going after her second choice for an interview, the bad-boy real estate tycoon, Ryan Malone.

RYAN MALONE HAD perfected the quick change from Sin's bodysuit nudity to tycoon tux. He'd broken every rule he'd ever made by continuing the conversation with the redhead after the curtain fell. But tonight seemed to be a night for change. Instead of leaving the theater as he'd always done, he was standing in the wings watching the reporter thread her way through the tables toward the reception area. Still more unsettled than he'd admit, he decided that Lottie was right. He'd be better off delaying his meeting with the woman he'd imagined he was making love to during his act. He'd told himself that his performance was merely a flirtation meant to show her she wasn't immune to Lord Sin's talents. Instead, without even trying, she'd turned the tables on him. That had never happened before.

Even Ryan knew that Lord Sin's last performance had been his best, for it had become a two-way seduction. That hadn't been an act. It had turned into a sexual tease that had left him totally shaken. What in hell had happened? And what was he going to do about it? What he wanted to do was find her, take her to his bed and make love to her in ways he'd only suggested. That couldn't happen. Lord Sin had closed up shop.

But—

Ryan Malone could.

Reeling from the aftermath of that thought, he moved quickly past the guests, toward the front entrance. He didn't know how he'd manage it, but tonight he was Ryan Malone the official representative of the Arts Council; he could do whatever he wanted later. He thought he'd avoided her when he felt someone touch his shoulder.

"Mr. Malone? I'm Sunny Clary, WTRU News. Will you give me a moment, please?"

Ryan turned. She was even more beautiful up close. Ripe, tangerine lips parted as she drew in a quick breath of air. She held out the mike with one hand and used the other to shove a tendril of red hair behind her ear. For a moment he allowed himself simply to look at her. Knowing that the camera was running, Ryan forced himself to focus on the future of the theater. Any seduction of Sunny Clary would have to wait until he was in better control. He smiled and said, "Of course. What may I tell you?"

Tell me? Tell me to remember this is business. To forget I've just been practically seduced by Lord Sin and that Ryan Malone is practically undressing me with his eyes. "Mr. Malone," Sunny began, trying to control the jitter in her voice, "you are not only a member of the Arts Council but you're also responsible for the events of the evening, the fund-raiser here tonight. Can you tell us how successful you were?"

"I understand that we did very well, but I only put the program together, Miss Clary. You'll have to give the credit for the idea to the man who donated the building for a Community Theater."

Stage fright was new to Sunny. She'd done plenty of interviews, but she'd usually been wearing slacks and she hadn't been twelve inches away from the ultimate Valentine heart-throb. "Of course." She smiled. "You're referring to the entertainer known as Lord Sin. A friend of yours, I believe?"

"We worked together on the program, yes," Ryan admitted, neatly turning her question into a benign statement.

"Like many of the women tonight, I have a rose that...someone gave me. Perhaps you'd like to explain its significance."

"Certainly. On Valentine's Day every lover gives his sweetheart a rose. In this case, the roses started at one hundred dollars. Most of our guests paid with a cheque, a very large check. I hope your gentleman was generous."

She turned over the check wrapped around the rose and gasped. Ten thousand dollars. "Oh, my goodness. Yes, the gentleman was more than generous. Will you tell our viewers what the money will be used for?"

"Renovating the building. But the work will take more than the money raised tonight. The entire community has to become involved. We hope members of your viewing audience will call the Arts Council and volunteer. Now, if you'll excuse me..." Ryan turned and started to walk away when he heard the reporter call out.

"Mr. Malone? Mr. Malone!" She hurried. "Will you please see that this check gets to the right person?"

He stopped and turned back, his mouth tight with the strain of walking away when what he wanted to do was throw the redhead over his shoulder and carry her out to his car and— Damn! He was losing it. Making Sunny Clary the recipient of his last performance had fired his hormones to killer proportions. He'd better get away before he revealed the state of his arousal. At that moment, his tormentor stumbled on a worn place in the carpet and reached out to steady herself. He had no choice but to catch her. Big mistake. He felt a jolt from his fingertips to the spot on his chest where her shoulder touched and straight down to his knees. He couldn't tell whether the gasp he heard came from him or her. "You seem a bit rocky," he finally said. "Did Lord Sin get to you, too?"

"Of course not," she protested a little too quickly as she stepped away. "It's the shoes and dress. I'm not used to wearing them."

His gaze flicked from her face to her feet and back. "Oh? Is nudity the dress code for WTRU?"

She shook him off. "I meant that I'm not used to three-inch heels and long dresses. I'm more the blue jeans type."

"Too bad. And I was thinking that WTRU had given new meaning to exposing the truth." His control was coming back. "Are you happy working there?"

"I'm happy. Or I will be if you'll let me interview you."

"Me? Why would you want to interview me, Miss Clary?"

She could have lied, made up some story about his being one of Atlanta's most eligible bachelors or she could have told him the real truth, that what she wanted was to fly off to some South Seas beach and spend hours making love in the moonlight. But, she remembered why she was here and went after a truth she could tell. "Actually you weren't my first choice. I wanted Lord Sin."

Ryan laughed. "I imagine most of the women here want Sin."

"Not wanted *him*. I wanted to *interview* him," Sunny insisted. "But he disappeared before I could get to him."

"Why would you be so intent on finding the man?" Ryan asked. "You really don't look like a woman who is attracted to male...dancers."

"I'm not. I'm a country girl. This is my first assignment for WTRU. Frankly, I consider this a fluff piece. I want to do more. But I have to prove myself. Revealing Lord Sin's true identity is my ticket out. If I find out who he is, I get transferred to investigative reporting."

Her eyes were green, not the emerald color of her dress

but something softer. Now they sparkled with the challenge Lottie was right. His attraction to this woman could be trouble. WTRU had a reputation for hiring people who went for the jugular. As innocent as she appeared to be, Sunny Clary would be a serious threat. If there was any way to tie Ryan Malone to Lord Sin, this woman might be the one to pull it off.

"And you want to report all the tough stuff?"

"Yes," she answered seriously. "I need an interview with Lord Sin. I'd really appreciate your assistance. Will you help me expose the man's identity?"

Ryan blinked. He'd been so caught up in wanting her body that he wasn't thinking clearly. Her innocence was dangerous. She drew you in before you realized you'd been caught. She was not going to just let Sin fade away. He would have to find a more public ending to make Lord Sin disappear forever. Suppose he let Sunny Clary write Sin's final story, the one Ryan Malone had created. Why not? *Sure, Malone, and you've got your spaceship anchored in the parking lot for your next mission to Mars.*

If the world learned that Ryan Malone earned his fortune from investments made as a stripper, he'd become the laughingstock of Atlanta. He had to get serious and find a way to stop her—quick. "Maybe I could help you. Let me get you a glass of champagne and we'll find a more private spot to talk."

"No champagne. I'm not much of a drinker. Couldn't we talk right here?" she asked, moving into an alcove off the lobby. "Just a minute." She reached down and slipped the back of a strappy sandal from her heel and kicked it off. The other soon followed. "Now, that's better."

Ryan clenched his teeth. Her long legs and her remark just blew off his newly gained control. He frowned. Misdirection, he decided. Put her on the defensive for a change. "I'm just curious. Most women love Lord Sin. Apparently he didn't seduce you."

"He tried. I guess I just didn't buy it," she lied. "Even years ago, this palace would have cost a bundle. He couldn't have made enough money stripping two nights a week to buy a building like this, could he?"

Ryan swallowed his impulse to tell her that not only could he, he had. And Lord Sin had owned a hotel and two restaurants as well, one of which he still owned on the Riviera. Instead, he said, "Sin doesn't call himself a stripper. And I'm told he owned several clubs—profitable ones."

"Where I come from, strippers only perform at the truck stops and they don't own them. Why did he keep his life secret if he had nothing to hide?"

"Maybe he had good reason," Ryan said. "Maybe dancing was the only way he could get what he wanted. What would you do to get what you wanted?"

She frowned, chewing the corner of her lower lip. "What do you mean?"

"You talk a good game, Ms. Clary. Tell me, have you ever cared about something so badly that you'd do anything to get it?"

"Yeah, the truth. But it cost me everything. This story will give it back."

"But you won't get it, Miss Clary, not without my help."

He watched her face as that thought churned in her mind. She seemed so sure of herself, so full if idealism. He couldn't believe that Sunny had ever been rejected. Not the way his mother had been. The pain of that rejection had killed her and driven him to succeed. Now he'd finally done what he'd set out to do. The dream would be fulfilled in two more weeks. The children's wing at Doctor's Hospital, named for his mother, would be dedicated. Then he could relax and enjoy his life as a successful businessman. And the only way to be sure of that was to make certain that Sunny Clary's zeal didn't interfere.

He leaned back against a fluted column and gave her a heated smile, intended to intimidate. "You say you want an interview with Lord Sin. What would you do to find him?"

His question stopped her for about ten seconds. "I'd do anything, so long as it's not illegal or immoral!"

Ryan didn't doubt for a minute that she meant it. But he was certain the "anything" that came to his mind was not what she was envisioning. In spite of the risk he was running, he was more intrigued with Sunny Clary than he had been with any woman in a long time. She'd put down the way he'd made his money and she doubted his success. Topping it off was her challenge, *"What's the matter? Aren't you up to seducing a real woman?"* Her taunt was still nagging at him. Lord Sin might not be up to seducing Sunny Clary, but Ryan Malone was. "Suppose I could arrange an interview?"

"Name your price."

Before he'd thought it out, he heard himself say, "I'll do what I can to help you find Lord Sin, if I can have you."

"Have?" Her voice quivered slightly. "Define have, from a legal and moral standpoint."

"Well, I'm not talking marriage so that covers legal. And moral? I'm not even certain morality exists anymore. But, hey, I'm a businessman turned lover, not a philosopher. What do I know?"

Sunny was taken with a bout of coughing. First her attraction to Lord Sin, now Ryan Malone was making her feel like she was in South Georgia on a riverbank in the middle of June. Hot. This was not what she'd learned in Journalism 101. "I think I will have that glass of champagne now."

He could tell she was delaying, looking for a way out. But he wasn't going to give her one. Once he'd made up his mind, having Sunny Clary felt right. Like a business deal

ipe for the taking. He told himself that burying Lord Sin for-
ver was all the justification he needed for the risk he was
aking to get Ms. Sunny Clary in bed. He deserved to have
ust one woman from all those Lord Sin had seduced over the
ears. He'd keep her so occupied with Ryan Malone that
he'd forget Sin. "Don't go away, Ms. Clary. I'll be right
back."

But he was saved from the necessity of leaving her by the
imely appearance of a waiter carrying a tray of slender
glasses still bubbling. Without taking his eyes off Sunny
Clary, he snagged two. Handing her a glass, he said, "I get
you and I'll try to persuade Lord Sin to grant your interview.
Are you game?"

"What makes you think *you* can do that?" she asked,
empted, in spite of the danger Malone represented. Her fa-
her would have said, "follow your instincts." She wondered
what her mother would have said if she'd lived to see her
daughter grow up.

"Let's just say, given the right situation, I might. I can't be
sure but I know some people who can help you."

"I'll have to think about it," she said, delaying her answer
again. How had she let herself get into this kind of situation?
Was the story worth the risk?

"Don't think too long." Malone warned. "I understand
Lord Sin is leaving town. You may only have a couple of
weeks."

She took a sip of her champagne, wrinkled her nose and
took another, seeking the courage she'd always heard came
from alcohol. It didn't come. "I can't imagine that you'd *want*
to sleep with me," she said desperately. "I'm just a country
girl."

"I'm not sure I believe that, and I don't sleep with women,
I make love to them."

She took another sip and realized her glass was empty. "And what exactly would you expect from me?"

"Some of your time, that's all."

"What about my job?"

"I won't interfere with that. In fact, if I talk to your boss, think he'll agree that spending time with me will get you some special stories. I think it's a win-win situation for both of us."

She was shaking her head, one finger tugging at an errant curl. "And what would you do? About us? About me?"

"Make love to you, of course."

"Ha!" The laugh was a bit shrill and ended immediately. "You can try," she said, frantically trying to find words that made her sound more in charge than she felt. "But, frankly Mr. Malone, you're just not Lord Sin."

Suddenly he leaned forward and kissed her. Just a light quick kiss that warmed the marble floor beneath her feet. She felt stunned for a moment, then held out her empty glass like some kind of shield. "Mr. Malone, I think I should tell you that my father is a minister who once served a prison term for a crime he didn't commit."

He took her glass, placed it along with his on a table beside them and said, "I think I should tell you that I never knew my father but he should have been in jail. Does that matter?"

She shook her head. "No, of course not. I didn't mean to offend you."

"You didn't. Shall we get back to our negotiations? You want Sin, I want you. We'll take it slow. We'll spend some time together. Two weeks ought to be just about enough time to give us both what we want."

"My father would say that I'd either have to accept your offer or 'cut bait and run.'"

"I think I'd like your father."

"Most people do. You're sure you've actually met Lord Sin face to face?"

"He and I had a face-to-face discussion about his performing before he finally gave in." Miss Clary didn't have to know the discussion took place via a mirror while he was shaving.

"If I were to agree—and I haven't yet—I'd insist on one little condition. During the next two weeks, you'll let me interview you. That way, if I don't find Sin, I'll still have a story."

"Oh, you'll have a story—even if you don't land Lord Sin," Ryan said, knowing that the thought of those red curls on satin sheets was clouding his vision. "I promise you that—lots of stories."

Sunny smiled, hesitantly at first, then more bravely. "Lord Sin doesn't have a chance." She reached down, picked up her shoes and turned to the exit, padding along as if she'd always gone barefoot in a formal dinner gown.

"Neither," he murmured to her retreating back, "do you."

3

THE STAFF WAS GEARING UP for the eleven o'clock wrap-up when Sunny stepped into the newsroom still wearing the slit-to-the-thigh green dress. A couple of wolf whistles were silenced by Walt's dry comment, "Be careful, guys, she's just been on the receiving end of Lord Sin's personal treatment followed by the Malone rush. We didn't have to drive the van back. We flew."

"Hush, Walt," Sunny said in exasperation, "or I'll tell them you got on the phone and talked dirty to your wife all the way home."

"Yeah," one of the announcers said, "and Pamela Anderson Lee is hot for my body."

"That's enough." Ted Fields, the news director, walked from his office into the main room. He gave Sunny a long look, stopping at the top of the split in her dress, and grinned. "When I hired a South Georgia reporter, I didn't know I'd found a sex goddess. Hold that skirt together and come in the office before I have to sweep up eyeballs."

"But what about editing the videotape?" she asked.

"Walt can handle it," was Ted's answer.

At Walt's nod, she followed Ted into his glass-enclosed office and sank down in the chair opposite his desk. "I hope I never have to do this again," she said, removing her shoes. "This isn't me. I'm the kind of girl who likes being barefoot—"

"I hope you're not going to say 'and pregnant,'" Ted said, perching on the side of his desk.

"I was going to say 'in the country.' I really am a country girl, or..." she added with a note of wistfulness in her voice "...I used to be." She twisted a tendril of auburn hair behind her ear. "If this assignment was some kind of kinky orientation, Mr. Fields, I hope I passed."

"Let me see the video and I'll let you know, and Sunny, call me Ted. I may be old enough to be your father, but I don't like to be reminded of it."

Rolling her eyes, Sunny sucked in a quick breath. "All right, *Ted*. It's just that I thought when I came to WTRU I'd be doing stories on real issues. I might as well have stayed in South Georgia. At least the drought and fire ants were life-altering events."

"Be patient, Sunny. This story on the theater is news, even without an interview with Lord Sin. I don't suppose you got a picture, did you?"

"I wish." Sunny rolled her shoulders and leaned her head back. "Oh sure. I got shots of the usual VIPs, the mayor and a couple of well-heeled contributors, but no Lord Sin."

"I didn't expect you to. If you'd managed to video him, the Sin Patrol would have confiscated it."

"Sin Patrol?"

"Just kidding, Sunny. So far as we know, Lord Sin has been squeaky clean. What about the interview with Malone?"

She gulped and wondered whether or not she should tell him the truth about Malone's offer, then decided that was personal—at least for now. "I did have a very strange conversation with the tycoon, but I didn't get to talk to him for very long. He's as complex as Lord Sin, and—" she added almost as an afterthought "—just as intriguing. He has promised me another interview, and possibly some inside stories—if I spend some time with him."

Her boss let out a dry laugh, eased himself off the desk and moved to his chair. "Sunny, I don't normally get involved in the personal life of my employees but I feel I ought to warn you. You're new in Atlanta and you don't know your way around yet. Ryan Malone is a pretty sophisticated guy, rarely seen with the same woman twice. He's known for being a two-week man. Although I like the idea of some inside stories, you're not ready for the Malone rush."

"I'm not a child, Ted, I'm a reporter. Malone has offered me a good deal."

"You sure you're not just caught up in Lord Sin's spell? I think the aging superstud got to you. My wife said he was...extraordinary, and she's not easy to impress."

"Aging? Boy, are you wrong. An old man could never have made the moves he did. He's pretty remarkable—if you like that kind of thing."

Ted smiled. "You're right. The first rule of a good journalist is to keep an open mind. Let yourself experience the event first. Then decide."

Experience the event? Sunny shivered. If she'd experienced any more, she'd have turned into a cinder in her seat of honor. "He's impressive, like one of those new-age magicians, alluring, mysterious and hypnotic. I think he graduated magna cum laude from the School of Lust. But I'm going to unmask him. And I'm going to use Ryan Malone to do it."

"I like it, Sunny."

"You do?"

"I do—but the station can't close down while you work on one story. I'll give you two weeks and you still have to take assignments."

"That's all I'll need," she assured him. "If I don't get something you'll like, I'll write promos and make the coffee."

"You're on. But remember what I said about Malone. I don't want you to miss opportunities but I don't want you to get hurt."

"Thanks, Ted."

"By the way, how's your coffee?"

"Lousy."

"That's what I thought. Now, go write your story."

She took a deep breath. Get hurt? She'd been there, done that and had the "I've Been Downsized" T-shirt to prove it. She didn't intend to let that happen again, either personally or as a reporter. "I don't want to be hurt either," she said softly.

Sunny stood, gathering her strappy shoes in one hand and holding herself upright by leaning on the desk with the other. She was physically drained. Thank goodness she wasn't one of the anchors who'd deliver her story. All she had to do was type the words to go along with Walt's shots.

"Hey, Sunny," someone called out, "better hustle, thirty minutes to air time."

"Thirty minutes?" She was a beginner on television, but she knew how to write a story. And she intended to get home in time to watch the story—only to see how well it looked.

She slid into a chair behind her desk and began to type.

The premier of *Gone With the Wind* at Atlanta's Rialto Theater in the thirties couldn't have been any more remarkable than the Valentine fund-raising gala held tonight at The Palace Of Sin, soon to become a community theater. But the star responsible, both for the donation of the building and the highlight of the evening's entertainment, is no Clark Gable. Instead, he is the internationally famous, golden-haired male stripper known as

Lord Sin. Tonight, Lord Sin packed the house with well-heeled contributors. This is to be his last performance. Now, here's our own Sunny Clary with more.

Sensational journalism, she decided, cheesy but attention-getting, as had been her dress. She hoped the story worked better than the slit in her skirt. On stage, Lord Sin had professed his desire for her but apparently it hadn't been enough for him to stick around for a more personal meeting. The only personal meeting she'd been invited to was by a dangerous real estate tycoon, Ryan Malone, who was sexy as sin and thought his father ought to have been in jail. At least he was honest if not honorable. He wanted her in his bed, and he'd told her that up-front. She'd never had a man be so blunt about his intentions, at least not at first. And she'd never been tempted to accept before.

But you're considering it, Sunny Clary. Malone is your means to an end. If you enjoy him a bit along the way, consider it one of the perks of the trade, like a parking space or a company car. Like the green dress and Ted's promise of a real assignment. Yeah...

She shook her head. It had to be the spell Lord Sin had put her under. She was thinking about him and Ryan Malone as if they were a dish of M&M's on her news desk. She'd just eat one. Then the bowl would be empty and she'd swear off sweets until the next deadline. Still, she was in the big time now and to succeed she'd have to be tough. She didn't have to give in to Ryan Malone if she didn't want to. She just had to let him try to seduce her.

Malone couldn't actually be serious about anything more than just getting to know her. He probably used that line about wanting her in his bed with all his dates. And she'd bet her last dollar that every one of them fell for it. He didn't know it, but she'd be the exception. Her career was at stake.

She'd win the bet. Using Ryan Malone to get to Lord Sin would be a challenge, but it would be fun. She could even turn the tables on him. What she wouldn't give to bring him to his knees.

Bad image, Sunny. The picture of Ryan Malone on his knees was one of the places she didn't want to go. She could only think of two things that came from a man kneeling before a woman, and a proposal wasn't the thing turning up her pulse.

"Whoa, girl! Let's get back to work." WTRU reported the news and she had about two minutes left to finish the story. Walt's opening shot was of the building, then he'd cut to her as she explained what the Arts Council had in store for the facility. The mayor would talk about the cultural offerings of the city and a few of the affluent Atlantans who turned out to make the building renovation possible. They'd close with her interview with Ryan Malone.

She ran a quick spell check and the story was timed and ready for broadcast. One of the advantages of being a local all-news station was that the story lineup was flexible, allowing for additions and changes at the last minute. If a story didn't get on one segment, it would be picked up on the next one, then it, or an update, would be repeated at thirty-minute intervals until the news was stale.

Still carrying her shoes, Sunny slid the strap of her evening purse over her shoulder and threaded her arms into her jacket as she made her way to the parking lot. Outside she stopped and looked up at the night sky. In South Georgia a million stars would have showered the night with brilliance. Here they paled in the city lights, but nothing could conceal the energy she felt. It seemed the very air, filled with new sounds and smells, promised new beginnings. She took a deep breath of cold air and felt a tingle of excitement raise goose bumps on her arms. Staying in the southern part of the state to be close to her father was no longer necessary. He'd gotten through his own tragedy. Now, as a minister, called late in life, he had his own church, made up of senior citizens who needed him. He'd let her go with his blessings and a promise to visit as soon as she was settled.

Leaving the newspaper had been harder; she felt as if she'd betrayed her neighbors when she was forced to suppress her biggest story "for the good of the community leaders." What she never mentioned was that leaving was, in some way, for her father, too. This new job was her chance to restore the integrity of the Clary name and she intended to do it. The one thing she wouldn't do again was conceal the truth, no matter whom it hurt.

With a shake of her shoulders, she opened the door to her loyal old Cutlass and crawled in. The first thing she'd do when she got her raise was buy a new car, one with heat. Leaving the small building that WTRU called home, she turned north on Peachtree, driving quickly, lest she miss the airing of her first story on her new job.

Atlanta was famous for its peach trees. Except the only peach trees she'd seen were streets and there were dozens of them: Peachtree Street, Road, Avenue, Hills, Drive and more. But the Atlanta landscape boasted dogwoods in the spring and magnolias in the summer—no peach trees. Now, in February, the worst month of the year, there were no blossoms and, except for the Georgia pines and magnolias, few leaves. Still, there was an energy about the city that made her want to run with the wind. Soon she'd check out the jogging trails at the nearest park.

Turning into the driveway that led to her new apartment which had been creatively described in the realtor's ad as a carriage house, Sunny smiled. It was a separate concrete block building constructed behind the house. At some point someone had used a pressure washer to blast away some of the layers of white paint, leaving a muted surface of old bricks on which the bare remains of rose vines and honeysuckle clung. She parked her car, climbed the steps to the upper quarters and went inside, flicking on the television just as the announcer introduced her story.

Walt was good. His camera work showed off the exotic decor of the building and caught the picture of affluence as the guests were served champagne and hors d'oeuvres.

Just as she slid out of the green dress and flopped down on her bed, plumping the pillows behind her head, the phone rang. Who would be calling her so late? "Hello?"

"This is Ryan Malone. I'm watching your story."

Damn him, she hadn't recovered from the last sensual onslaught. It wasn't fair of him to invade her private sanctuary without warning. "How'd you get my number?"

"From the guest list. Your employer must have filled out the form for you."

"Remind me to tell them not to do that again."

"Doesn't matter. I have it now."

The camera was sweeping the reception, panning the mayor and his party, then, it moved across the lobby to the two people standing near the exit, a tall redhead in green and a dark-eyed, intense man in a tux.

"That's some dress," he said.

"Best free air time could be traded for," she quipped. "I suppose your tux is custom-made, isn't it?" Dumb, Sunny. It wasn't the tux, it was what was underneath it that made her quiver like an adolescent.

"It is. Does that bother you that my tux is custom fitted?"

"Of course not. It's just that like you, Lord Sin, this kind of thing isn't the real me. I'm not accustomed to dealing with men like you."

"We're just men, Sunny."

"Yeah, and I'm just a woman, a woman who never owned a dress like that."

"Personally, I think the green dress was the real you. Of course, I don't know what you're wearing now."

She glanced guiltily down at her nude body, at nipples dusky rose and erect and felt a hot flush spread across her cheeks. "And you're not going to. Have you called Lord Sin?"

"I'm working on it."

"I wasn't sure you were really serious," she said.

"Oh, but I was. I can see that I'm going to have to teach you how to play the game."

"And this is a game?"

"Of course. We've already set the stakes. I have two weeks to get you in my bed."

"No, you have two weeks to try. In the meantime you're going to set me up with Lord Sin and I get to interview you along the way."

"I'm going to try, but only if you're trustworthy."

"I'm trustworthy. I was a Girl Scout and Girl Scouts never tell a lie."

"Then tell me we have a deal."

There was a long silence where nothing but the sound of breathing filled the phone lines. Finally, she took a deep breath and said softly, "I won't say okay to you taking me to bed, but if that's your offer, I'm willing to let you try."

"Good. Now, tell me what you're wearing."

"I will not."

"In that case, I'll create my own fantasy. I'd say your bed is covered in white satin sheets and, since you just got home, you're still wearing what you were wearing underneath that green dress."

She smiled, allowing herself to enjoy his teasing. "Oh, and what is that?"

"Nothing. Nothing except a suntan. How am I doing so far?"

She swallowed hard. "Missed by a mile. My bottom sheet is burgundy stretch knit and there isn't a top sheet, just a comforter."

He laughed. "You're wrong, darling. It's my fantasy and I'll create it any way I like. Don't you want to know what I'm wearing?"

"I do not. I'm going to hang up now, Mr. Malone. Phone sex isn't my thing."

"Nor is it mine, but it's as close as I can come to experiencing the real thing tonight. But that will change. Tomorrow I'm going out to buy knit sheets and a comforter. Just tell me what you like. As a lover, I aim to please."

Forget the telephone and modern conveniences like beds, she thought. They might as well have been alone in the tent of some Bedouin sheikh. Obviously Malone was a man who let nothing come between him and what he was doing. And what he was doing was seducing her, word by word, image by image. Even if the words weren't whispered in that erotic, spellbinding rasp of Lord Sin, the husky timbre of Malone's voice set her breathing aflutter. She sucked in a deep breath and turned off the television. The silence was worse.

"Tell me, Sunny, what do you want?"

"I'd like to meet Lord Sin."

"You're impatient, too, aren't you?"

"Always," Sunny agreed. "You can never count on having enough time later. So for me, there is no later—only now."

"Oh, but there's always later. There has to be. A person needs the promise of tomorrow. You use today to fulfill that promise."

Sunny shifted the phone to her other shoulder, glad to substitute a good argument for the sex talk Malone seemed intent on engaging in. "Not me, Mr. Malone. I'll take today.

It's right here. I can touch it, feel it, use it. Tomorrow? I don'
trust the hussie."

"You have an interesting philosophy," he said. "One tha
gives a reporter permission to expose, to bully, to abuse
even to be dishonest."

"Sometimes you have to. Otherwise, given enough powe
and time, the truth can be withheld."

There was a long pause. "And sometimes there are rea
sons to withhold the truth," he said in a low voice. "But fo
now I'm going to take a page out of your book and use to
day—tonight—to get started."

"Get started? On what?"

"On getting you into my bed."

The man had a one-track mind. "That is not a done deal.
told you, you can try."

"But you've been thinking about it, haven't you?"

She squirmed and held her breath. She'd thought about lit
tle else. Even caught up in his fantasy, a tiny grain of logi
still held. How could she be so acutely responsive to two
men? Lord Sin was the fantasy, the unknown dream lover
But Ryan Malone was real. Thinking about him? If he coul
see her, the color of her cheeks would be a dead giveaway
"No. I've been busy," she lied.

"I don't believe you."

"Then you must be the most conceited man in the state
Besides, I'm beginning to wonder if you really can get m
close to Lord Sin."

"I can get you close."

"When?"

Ryan let the seconds tick away as if he were formulating
his answer. "When you prove yourself trustworthy."

That stopped her. She wasn't prepared for the seriousnes
of his answer. That was the second time he'd mentioned be
ing trustworthy. What had happened to Lord Sin to mak

truth the most important thing in his life? Or was it Ryan who was so cautious? Finally, she answered. "You don't know me, Malone, but if you did you'd understand that no one puts a higher value on trust than I do. It comes second only to commitment to the truth."

"I hope you're right, Sunny Clary. I'll pick you up at the television station at three o'clock tomorrow."

"Where are we going?"

"To get you one of those inside stories, at a birthday party."

"Whose birthday party?"

"You ask too many questions," he said.

"I'm a reporter," she argued, "a good one. Or I will be. Asking questions is what I do best."

"I don't know who licked the red off your candy," Ryan said in exasperation, "but I wish you'd stop bristling and go along with me. It will be worth it."

Licked the red off your candy? That didn't sound like a sophisticated business tycoon. To elicit that kind of reaction, she knew she'd gone too far. But she couldn't let the man run over her. "You forget, Mr. Malone, even if I did agree to go to a party, I have a job."

"The party will be part of your job. I called Fields."

"You did what?" He'd said he'd give her stories, but this wasn't what she'd expected. And to call her boss before he'd discussed it with her was inexcusable. "Malone, I'll decide what stories I cover."

"You don't have to bring a gift," he went on as if she hadn't spoken. "That's already been taken care of. One hundred red roses."

Sunny couldn't resist. "Were they wrapped in a check?"

"Well, yes, they were."

"From you or Lord Sin?"

"Does it matter?"

It mattered, she told herself. Attending a party with Malone was much too disturbing. But if it would get her closer to Lord Sin, she couldn't afford to pass it up. "Just checking the facts, WTRU's first rule of journalism," she said. "The second is to tell the truth."

"Is it? I don't think I believe that," he said dryly.

Malone's conversation was taking a serious turn she hadn't expected. "It is for me."

"As a reporter, do you always tell the truth?"

This time it was Sunny's time to hesitate. "When I'm allowed."

"Good. Tell me, what are you wearing?"

She glanced down at her body and watched her nipples turn into dusky rose-colored berries. "Excuse me?"

"I said, tell me what you're wearing."

"Perfume and a smile," she replied and hung up the phone.

Ten seconds later it rang. He was laughing. "What kind? And where do you put it?"

Before Sunny could throw the phone across the room, it went dead. Ryan Malone was obviously taking lessons from Lord Sin. Excite, titillate and leave the object of your attention panting in the dark.

It was working. Every part of her seemed to be shivering, pulling in a different direction. She pulled on a faded Miami Dolphins T-shirt, hoping to erase the tingling sensation of her bare body against her sheets. It didn't work. She ought to just sleep in the green satin dinner gown. There'd be no friction there. The infamous dress lay puddled on the floor like a melted lollipop. Melted. She'd got that right. Still flushed and totally frustrated, she grabbed the dress, hung it in her closet out of sight and climbed into her bed. Switching off the light, she lay in the darkness.

Back home, as she unwound, she'd have heard the night

birds calling, or the occasional wail of a coon dog hot on the trail of a wild animal. She felt a little like that animal. Winded, out of breath and being pursued.

Overstimulated from the excitement of the evening, she felt as if she were hurtling through the darkness in fast forward. Facing down hardened criminals or politicians under fire couldn't be as difficult as the emotional turmoil she'd been through tonight, first as the object of Lord Sin's attention, then Ryan Malone's, the two sexiest men in Atlanta.

She came to her feet and moved to the window. Here she only heard the sound of traffic, an occasional car horn and the scrape of a branch against her windowpane. She leaned her forehead on the glass and wished she could pick up the phone and call...whom? There was no one she could talk to about this. She was alone, just as she'd been ever since her father had gone to jail. She'd lost him for a time to depression and despair. Even now that they were past that, things were not the same. She was still his daughter, but she wasn't his little girl anymore.

The phone rang again.

Sunny grabbed the receiver. "Now listen to me. If you don't let me get some sleep I'll spend the next two weeks in my own bed—alone."

It was Ted Fields's amused voice that said, "I'd say that's the smart thing to do. But I need you at the station tomorrow and I think Walt's going to have a hard time pushing your bed up Peachtree Street."

She closed her eyes and counted to ten before she said, "Malone called you."

"He did. But you don't have to go. I could always send you and Walt to cover the Southlake Mall beauty contest instead. They'll be crowning a Sweetheart of Love in three age groups, starting with the toddlers."

Sunny groaned. "First a stripper, then a beauty contest for rug rats. Please, Ted, give me something with teeth."

"Sorry. If you're looking for teeth, I don't think this birthday party will qualify. Unless you're willing to accept the false kind. The youngest guests will probably be in their sixties."

"Senior citizens?" Sunny groaned. "Why are you doing this to me?"

"Because Malone asked for you and Malone is good news. I'll see you in the morning, Sunny, but I'm sending you to the retirement home tomorrow afternoon—with Walt. If you want to go home with Malone, it's up to you."

"It's a conspiracy. I came here to expose corruption and you're shipping me off to an old folks' home for tea and crumpets. I suppose you have instructions on what I should wear?"

"No. You made a good choice the last time, I'll leave your wardrobe up to you."

"Fine. But I'll need to be a few minutes late in the morning. I have to do some quick shopping."

"Shopping?" Ted said, his voice a bit puzzled. "You're not going for a wheelchair are you? Having Walt push your bed was a joke."

"Don't worry, Ted. You can trust me not to embarrass you. I'm the Good-News Girl, remember? At least until I get my big story."

At least Ted's call took care of her decision. He'd made it for her. But in her gut she'd known she would have gone with Malone anyway. She was glad Ted hadn't forced her to be specific about her shopping expedition. He'd never understand why she was buying sheets, plain, white cotton sheets with old-fashioned lace on the hem. She didn't intend to allow Ryan Malone to ever see her bed, but knowing that she'd destroyed whatever new fantasy he was creating would make her feel as if she'd won her first skirmish.

She went to her closet and considered what she *would* wear. No more green dresses. Tomorrow Sunny Clary would be strictly business, from the inside out.

Tomorrow she'd be dressed in black. And, this time, the dress wouldn't be all she was wearing.

4

LORD SIN CAME TO HER in the night. One minute there was only sweet sleep. The next, he slid beneath the covers and covered her mouth with his kisses, and her body with his own, his hand sliding beneath her and holding her close. Sunny groaned. Even in the dream, and she knew it was a dream, she recognized him, as if she'd been waiting. Her pulse raced. Her thighs opened, welcoming him, but he held back. He simply looked down at her, whispering in that incredibly sexy voice. She didn't know what he was saying, she only knew that he'd come in the darkest hour as he'd promised.

Had she wished him there? She didn't know. His lips touched hers once more, tracing the edges then moving over them, claiming them masterfully. She moaned again and pulled him closer, her fingers lacing themselves behind his head and holding him. She couldn't see his eyes but she wanted to. Were they the kind of clear hot blue that pressed the heat of the sun against white beaches, the color of clear tropical water that made her think of hot sex?

Or were they Malone's midnight-black, flashing with tempered amusement and the promise of inner fire? Were the hands touching her part of his planned seduction? Could she refuse?

"Who are you?" she finally managed to whisper.

"Does it matter?" A tendril of hair tickled her cheek as he shifted his position to plant little kisses down her neck and over her breast. She felt her nipple harden as he took it in his mouth.

"I'm here for you now," he whispered. "All you had to do was ask."

"But I didn't—"

"Yes. You did." He moved beneath her T-shirt and caressed her breast. "You need me, Sunny. You don't have to be alone." And for a moment the tenderness in his voice overwhelmed her.

How could he know about loneliness, about how abandoned she'd felt at twelve when her mother died, then later when her father went to prison? She didn't answer. She couldn't. Desperately, she pressed herself against him, felt his hardness, the hardness he was denying her. "Please, Lord Sin."

"Not yet," he whispered. "But soon." He raised himself up. She tensed and waited, her body throbbing with desire. Then, like a thief in the night, he was gone.

Her eyes flew open. She was alone in her own bed, with the sunlight pouring through her window and drenching her with winter warmth. The experience had all been an erotic dream. One that left her incredibly aroused.

Still shaken, she rubbed her eyes, then glanced at the clock radio on the table beside her bed. Eight o'clock. She forced herself to sit up, stumbled to the shower and turned on the hot water. Last night she'd been completely drained after her encounter with Lord Sin. Then Ryan Malone had called, stirring her unsettled emotions even further. No wonder she'd had such an erotic dream. It could have happened to anyone, she told herself. Except it had never before happened to her.

If Sunny Clary were forced to answer in a court of law, she couldn't have said with certainty who her night visitor was. Lord Sin or Ryan Malone or some fantasy lover she'd created in her mind. She just knew she had to take control of her

emotions. But first, she had to get over this incredible desire
Ted Fields had given her the chance of a lifetime, but she'd
have to earn her acceptance, establish her credibility in At
lanta if she intended to become an investigative reporter
And being late wouldn't make a good impression. Stripping
off her T-shirt, she turned the hot water to cold and stepped
in. This morning she understood the benefit of a cold
shower.

Minutes later her body was an icicle and she was furious
with herself for letting a man, any man, bring her to such a
state. She was no inexperienced virgin. Not that she was
wanton. She'd thought she was in love at seventeen, talked
herself into being in love at twenty-two and had a few unsat
isfactory encounters in between. But since her last budding
relationship ended, she'd sworn to put her career first—even
if there were times she wished there were someone to share
it with. But not like this—not through a relationship with a
phantom lover.

Mass hypnosis, that's what it was. Lord Sin's voice
through that microphone had some kind of lingering sublim
inal effect on her. She didn't know how it worked but tha
had to be the answer. Then Ryan Malone, with his bad-boy
charm, continued the seduction with his absurd claim that he
wanted her in his bed. He'd recognized and used her deter
mination to find Lord Sin to try and seduce her. That
shouldn't have been a surprise; she knew he liked women
But why her? In spite of the way she'd presented herself last
night, she wasn't that kind of woman. She was a profes
sional, even if she was a small-town girl.

And today she had to make him understand that.

Thirty minutes later, with a generous helping of gel, she'd
forced her unruly hair into a severe twist, applied a light
smattering of makeup and donned sensible undergarments
a serious black suit, hose and heels. If there was a wake or a

funeral to cover, she was Ted's girl. At the last minute, re-membering that they were going to a birthday party, she added a hummingbird pin to her lapel. On her way to the car, the red and green stones in its wings caught the sunlight and glittered like fire. *Bad idea, Sunny. Serious, dedicated, pro-fessional, that's what you are today. No froufrous. Nothing to sug-gest gaiety today.* She started to unfasten the pin then changed her mind. The party and Ryan Malone were six hours away.

At a nearby department store, she found simple cotton sheets. They didn't fit her personality but they would serve the purpose of proving to herself and to Ryan Malone, should the situation ever arrive, that she wasn't what he imagined her to be. A surprising chunk of her first paycheck later and she was headed for the TV station, only a few minutes late. The receptionist gave her a serious once-over. "Ah, phooey," she said with mock regret, "you're not wear-ing the green dress."

"Sorry," Sunny said with a forced smile. "Cinderella has turned back into a scullery maid."

"Ah, but for one night, she *was* Cinderella," the reception-ist said wistfully. "And, don't tell Teddy, but the switch-board lit up like a Christmas tree last night with viewers wanting to know who the redhead was."

"Lord Sin wanna-bes, no doubt" was her resigned reply.

There was no funeral to be covered, not even a political speech. In fact she spent most of the morning on the phone getting and verifying facts for follow-ups on stories they'd already told. A few inquiries about inside sources in city government were met by the other staff members with chilly response. Finally when the take-out lunch she'd ordered ar-rived, she went to the station archives, beginning five years ago. If she hoped to uncover wrongdoing in the present, she had to know who'd done what in the past. And in the city of Atlanta, there were a lot of people reported to be doing a lot

of things, including Ryan Malone. She discovered that as one
of the up-and-coming movers and shakers, he'd been ap-
pointed by the mayor to a committee charged with bringing
Atlanta to the attention of the world. There was plenty of information on Malone, mostly about his business transactions
and his humanitarian activities, but little about the man himself. The only personal fact she knew about him was that he
didn't know his father. And there was no mention of one in
the files.

Another story announced the closing of an old Atlanta
landmark, the adult entertainment club, The Palace Of Sin.
Sunny wondered briefly how Lord Sin and Malone had ever
crossed paths, unless Malone had been one of the palace's
regular patrons. He didn't strike her as the kind of man
who'd frequent The Palace Of Sin. Ryan Malone seemed to
live his life in the public eye. A more logical scenario was
that he had reached Lord Sin through Miss Lottie Lamour
like everyone else. Either that or this entire game, as he'd
called it, was a complete hoax instigated to bring her to his
bed. The more she thought about it, the more likely that idea
seemed.

THERE WAS NOTHING EASY about Ryan Malone's morning, beginning with a telephone call from Lottie. "All right, Ryan,
tell me about it. What kind of situation did you get yourself
into?"

"Situation? I don't know what you're talking about."

"Hah! I saw you in the lobby last night, playing up to that
reporter. I warned you, you're going to blow your cover."

"I am not blowing my cover," he snapped. "Besides, I've
been giving some thought to revealing the truth." He hadn't
been, but now that he'd said it, the idea wasn't bad. "Not the
real truth, of course, but one I've created. If I handle it right,
Lord Sin won't be able to hurt me."

"You can't be serious."

"But I am. Sooner or later, someone could go after the truth, maybe find out that Lord Sin is really named Jack Ivy. Maybe I could let Sunny Clary be the one. I'll give her a trail to Jack and let her tell the world who Sin is. Then they both disappear."

"You're just trying to give yourself a reason to be with her. You're talking with your hormones, not your mind. I knew you'd run into a woman you couldn't manipulate one day, but I never thought she'd curl your hair like this one has."

"Sunny Clary isn't curling my hair or manipulating me or anything else," he snapped. Ryan didn't want to admit to himself that he wasn't so much angry with Lottie as he was annoyed at himself for revealing to Sunny information about his father. He still didn't know why he'd done it.

"Then why are you so cross?"

"I'm not cross! I just didn't get much sleep."

When he'd finally slept he'd dreamed of wild sex and rejection. He'd known at the time whom he was making love to but once he woke, it all vanished. As a child he'd had terrible dreams that he'd carried around with him, dreams that tortured him until he finally learned to forget. Forget, not only the dreams, but the life he'd had to live in the foster homes where he stayed until he was sixteen. That's when he'd run away, determined to fend for himself. He shuddered now to think of what might have happened to him if he hadn't met Lottie who hired him as a part-time janitor at the club where she served as wardrobe mistress and general mother hen to the dancers. She'd taken him home to live with her, then sent him back to finish high school. And later, college. She'd been there for him, but she wasn't his mother. His mother had given him up when he was five.

"And why didn't you sleep?" Lottie asked, the tone of her voice saying that she already knew why. "Don't try to fool

me. That redhead's twisted your shorts. I knew it the minute
I saw her. It's all because she turned you down, isn't it. Now
you're hooked on the chase like a bull after a cow."

"Lottie, I hope you didn't talk to her like this last night."

"Of course not, boy. I talked real good, just like one o
those *highbrow ladies* in the audience. I taught you how to
perform and you taught me how to be classy. But you know
it as well as me: being a performer was a lot more than
being a stuffy businessman."

Ryan sighed. After his wild dreams of making love to
Sunny, he'd spent the rest of the night pacing. *Fun? Yes. Bu*
the curtain came down and Lord Sin went home alone. It had
taken years of careful planning to create Ryan Malone, respected businessman—fourteen years. He'd wined, dined
and even bedded a few women, but he'd been afraid to let
himself get too close to one. So he always ended the relationships before that happened. Living a secret life had taken its
toll.

Then he'd taken one look at a sassy, sexy reporter and he
was doing his best to throw everything he'd accomplished
right out the window.

He knew he should listen to Lottie. From the beginning,
she'd been his rock and he'd become the son she never had.
Still, sometimes Lottie went too far. Like now.

"And another thing, Ryan," she was saying, "I seriously
think you ought to get married. You've got too many moth-
ers and no wife."

He groaned. "I don't want to get married."

"Why? I'd get married in a heartbeat if I could find some
rich dude who could still get it up."

Ryan laughed, teasing her as always. "Lottie, you're a
sixty-five-year-old woman with everything you want. What
would you do with a husband?"

"I've got a few rabbits left in my hat and I'd like a man to make a little magic with, sonny."

Sunny. All it took was hearing her name. Lottie had just undone any good she'd accomplished with her phone call and she didn't even know it. Still, she'd forced him to marshal his thoughts. "Lottie, I want to bring her to see you."

"You want to do what? I thought you were listening, but apparently you weren't. She's dynamite, ready to explode and you're the match. And you're going to get burned by her fallout."

"I certainly hope so" was the comment he made under his breath. "Lottie, listen. Think about it. Using Ms. Clary to kill Lord Sin once and for all is a smart idea. And I want *you* to tell her the story we planned."

"You think she's going to believe that he's gone to the Riviera where he lives like a king on his millions? Well I don't. It might fly for the dummies in your audience but not under that redhead's scrutiny."

"You're right. I'm going to have to give her proof. She's an investigative reporter so I've come up with a way for her to get the truth, at least the truth as I've arranged it. I'm taking her to Isabella's birthday party. Isabella will tell her that she'll put in a word with Lord Sin."

"And you don't think this smart reporter will think it a little odd that you're friends with two ex-strippers?"

"No, she'll just think that Ryan Malone has a wide range of investments, including Rainbow House."

"Forget about her, Ryan," Lottie pleaded. "Taking her there is a mistake. Give it up. Don't see her again."

"I don't seem to be able to do that," he admitted. "She's a very intriguing woman."

"It's her body you don't want to give up," Lottie snapped. "You're having a mid-life crisis and you're not even forty. Listen to me, loverboy, I'm going to tell you what to do. Go buy yourself one of those plastic blow-up lady dolls, the life-like kind, and put a red wig on it."

"What makes you think a blow-up lady doll would work?" he asked, laughing.

"Well, the boy dolls do."

RAINBOW HOUSE WAS the most elegant retirement home Sunny had ever seen. The dreamy lyrics of Guy Lombardo wafted from the ballroom off the lobby and she could see people dancing, senior citizens. A muscular young man in jeans and a T-shirt greeted her from the reception desk. "Hello, you're Sunny Clary. Welcome."

"Well...yes, I am. And thank you. My photographer will be here in just a moment. We're here to meet—"

"Ryan. I know. He said to bring you right in. Miss Isabella is pretending she's upset because you're going to videotape her party. But she isn't. She's been saving her strength for this afternoon."

Sunny watched Walt come through the doors, take one look around and roll his eyes in dismay. "If she really doesn't want to be on television, we don't have to do this," Sunny said to the receptionist.

"Oh, she's excited about being on TV. Isabella is an old pro. She just doesn't want anyone to know how old she is. She hates her wheelchair, but she tires easily. Come on, I'll take you to Ryan and the others."

Inside the ballroom, beneath an arbor decorated with greenery and red roses, Sunny spotted the guest of honor among the guests. She was wearing a turn-of-the-century lace dress with a narrow waist, a slim skirt and a flare at the bottom. The crown and the scepter she carried completed the regal look. But there was something about the twinkle in her eyes that warned Sunny she might not be what she appeared. Miss Isabella would have been right at home on the

Titanic. She could have *been* on the Titanic. She had to be a hundred years old.

"Miss Clary!" Ryan Malone walked toward her, his long stride pulling his jeans tight against long slim legs, making her think about her dream. He nodded at Walt, gave her a long, amused look, then asked, "Do you think that will make a difference?"

"What?"

"The change in your appearance? Sometimes being concealed is more appealing than being exposed."

"It's you who likes fantasies. I prefer the real thing. And what you see is what you get."

He lifted one dark, wicked eyebrow. "Oh? When?"

She frowned. Though Walt hung back, pretending to ignore the conversation, something about Malone made her words come out wrong and she actually blushed. "I thought this was a party," she said. "Aren't you going to introduce me to the birthday girl?"

He glanced indulgently at the older woman who wasn't even trying to conceal her impatience. "I'd better or she's going to crack my head with her baton."

Sunny took another look at the honoree. Her crown looked like the real thing but her throne was a wheelchair and the scepter actually was a baton. "Don't tell me she was a cheerleader."

"Well, she was an entertainer. Isabella, this is Sunny Clary. Sunny, Isabella is a friend of Lord Sin's."

"I saw you on TV last night. Reminded me of myself a few years ago. Course, you might want to avoid the wind in that dress you were wearing. You'd look great on stage but those folks at the party you were attending might be a little prissy."

Sunny couldn't hold back a smile. She was going to like Isabella. "Thank you for inviting me to your party," she said.

"Walt—" she nodded at her cameraman who'd come up behind "—is a genius with a camera. I hope you'll let him tape the party for the viewers of WTRU."

"I'd love it. But why would anybody want to watch me and my party when they can see Madonna on MTV?" She laughed. "I would have said Blondie but that would show I'm not up to date, wouldn't it?"

Ryan let go of Sunny's arm and walked over to Isabella to drop a quick kiss on her forehead. "You're never behind the times, Belle. Listen, I think they're playing our song. Would you care to dance?"

The music was supplied by a disc jockey who played records on request. The song was an old ballad. Sunny remembered the melody, but not the words. Ryan had waited until the tune was half done before he held out his hand.

"I would indeed, you rascal, but you know that's not my kind of music. I like something with a beat."

"Well, I like something slower and romantic."

"If you want romance, Ryan," she said as she took his hand, "you're asking the wrong girl to dance."

Sunny nodded to Walt. "Get this." She'd videotape an intro back at the station once she had a better handle on the story. The guy from the reception desk came and stood beside Sunny. She watched as Malone led the elderly woman slowly around the floor. He was a very good dancer, a rarity in today's world. Malone did most of the moving and he did it in such a way that Isabella didn't have to. Sunny had to admit that his brand of gallantry was as seductive as Lord Sin's elaborate performance, and just as magical.

The other dancers gradually stopped and moved back to watch. As the floor cleared, Sunny realized that among the party-goers, there were a number of well-built older men wearing jeans and T-shirts. "Are all these men employed by the center?" she asked.

"Yes. Most of our residents are women and they get tired of each other. Mr. Malone came up with this idea of hiring senior citizens and a few college kids to supplement the women caregivers. It seems to work well."

Sunny smiled. "I'll bet the ladies like that."

The boy gave her a wide grin. "Some of them like it a little too well."

It took Sunny a moment to understand what he meant. She rolled her eyes and pulled out her notepad. Was every story she was covering going to turn into some documentary on sex? "What's your name? And how long have you been here?"

"I'm Ron. I've been here two years—one more 'til graduation, then I'll be a physical therapist." He grinned. "The ladies like that and I like the money."

"It sounds as if you're some kind of gigolo for hire." She stared at him stonily. "Exactly what kind of therapy are you offering them?"

Ron's expression narrowed. "You misunderstand, Ms. Clary. I meant that physical therapy and exercise are a valuable part of our service. As you can see, our ladies are in remarkably good shape and that's all due to Ryan Malone's generosity."

To cover her embarrassment over the implied insult she'd just given, Sunny studied her notes, then said, "I'm sorry. I've had a rather unusual introduction to my job but I had no right to let that carry over to this assignment. You said Mr. Malone came up with the idea to hire men. Does he own Rainbow House?"

"One of his companies does."

"None of this makes any sense." When she realized that Ron was frowning, she changed directions. No point in making an enemy. "Can you give me the guest of honor's full name?"

"Isabella Giovanna." He told Sunny that Isabella had come to Rainbow House right after the facility changed owners, two years ago. "Since then, the improvements have been amazing. All the ladies have to do is mention something to Isabella and the next thing we know, it's done. Mr. Malone is a remarkably generous man."

She'd tried not to look at Ryan admiringly but it was hard. Short of making a spectacle of herself, she had run out of excuses not to watch. He was wearing a blue chambray shirt with the hip-hugging jeans and a tweed jacket. He was a real, breath-stealing soap opera bad boy; he was also a mystery. His good deeds were extolled in every newspaper, along with pictures of him and whichever lady he was escorting for the evening. But she'd seen nothing about Rainbow House and no mention was ever made of a family or a past.

Maybe Isabella was a relative. Watching her move, Sunny decided she must have been a showgirl, too. Maybe she was a friend of Lottie. Or Lord Sin. Then it made sense. Malone had brought her here because Isabella knew Lord Sin.

Malone looked at her and smiled, then looked away. *He just glanced at you, Sunny.* She had no excuse for the breathless feeling that temporarily cut off her air flow. With the hand he had placed behind Isabella's back he motioned to the master of ceremonies to end the song and for someone to bring Belle's chair. The music stopped and, as if he were escorting a real princess, Malone brought Isabella to the center of the floor where Ron waited with her chair.

"Isabella is going to entertain us now," Malone said. "Ms. Clary, you might want to get this on tape."

"Of course she'll tape it," Isabella quipped, "but five will get you ten, the station won't run it."

"Why wouldn't we run it?" Sunny asked.

A spotlight circled Isabella and the other lights were dimmed. Walt stepped forward. Isabella steadied herself with one hand atop the back of her chair and began. With surprisingly nimble fingers, Isabella twirled her baton. But it was what she did next that brought the party-goers to their feet. "I'll show you. Turn off that camera, young man. This is private." When he'd complied, she tossed the baton aside, batted her false eyelashes and began to recite a limerick, accented with exaggerated eye movements, bumps and grinds.

"There once was a man named Lord Sin,
Who was my personal friend.
I taught him his moves,
From his eyes to his....shoes.
Now that he's gone we have to pretend."

She lifted her baton and became Carrie Nation.

"So lift a glass, my ladies, for the man we've lost.
Let's all unite, say a prayer tonight.
Send us more sin...
We all need Sin. Amen."

She bowed her head reverently. Her voice was thready but coy. And when she burst out laughing at the shock on the faces of the guests, Sunny knew she'd met a jewel. "So I'm no poet," Isabella chuckled. "I'm a dancer and I know my men, both of them."

Sunny couldn't stop herself from smiling. This was a woman who knew performing, how to capture an audience. As Isabella sat down, she gave Sunny a wink and Sunny understood instinctively that Isabella truly did know Lord Sin. That Malone was living up to his part of their bargain and Isabella just might put in a good word for her with Sin. But it wasn't just his help she appreciated. Any man who befriended lonely old ladies couldn't be all bad. It took her a few minutes to figure out she was thinking about Malone—not Lord Sin. She was confused.

And she refused to consider her part of their bargain.

The residents and guests applauded and Isabella blew a kiss. "Now, Ryan, you naughty boy, dance with your girl while I catch my breath."

His girl? What had Malone told Isabella? Sunny took a quick step back. "Sorry. I'm working."

"Nonsense," Isabella said. "This is a party, my party and everyone here has to dance."

"I'm not his girl, Ms. Giovanna," Sunny protested. How in hell had she allowed this to get all turned around? The focus of the story was Isabella and the retirement home—not Sunny and Ryan or Lord Sin. Even a first-year reporter knew that the press didn't interact personally with the public.

"It's your birthday. That makes your wish my command, Belle," Malone said, and pulled Sunny onto the floor.

"Don't do this, Malone. Walt, don't you dare video this."

"Don't worry, dear," Isabella said. "There's no reason you can't have a little fun. If your employer is that much of a Simon Legree maybe you ought to find another job. You know everyone in Atlanta, Ryan. Pull some strings."

Sunny's protest fell on deaf ears. She was tall, but Malone was taller and he was stronger, too. She glanced up at jet-black eyes and they turned up the heat she'd already felt when he'd taken her hand. "I think you ought to know. I've got you figured out," she said, "and this isn't going to work."

"Oh? And what have you figured out?"

"It's obvious that Isabella is another friend of Lord Sin's. Isn't she?"

"Yes."

"You want me to believe that Lord Sin is a kind and generous man who deserves his privacy."

"He is."

"And you want me to accept your motives as being just as pure. What I think is you're a kind of emotional con artist, and this way of doing things isn't going to work with me. My father trusted people. I don't."

"Tell me about your father. Are you close?"

"Now we are. After my mother died, he threw himself into his work. He didn't know how scared I was. I know now he was scared, too."

"Who looked after you?"

"Well—nobody. I was twelve and I looked after myself."

"But you missed him, didn't you?"

"I was lonely," she admitted, that confession coming out of the blue. She'd never let anyone know that—not even her father—not even during her monthly visits to the prison where he'd been confined. By that time she was in college and she didn't want to worry him.

"I know about being lonely," Ryan said. "But don't worry, you don't have to be lonely anymore. You have me."

He pulled her closer. She stepped on his foot and was rewarded with a groan. "What's the matter, Ms. Clary? Didn't you ever learn to dance?"

"Oh, I learned but like most people, my dancing was learned to the beat of groups like the B-52s and REM," she shot back. "In other words, I don't waltz. Where'd you learn to dance? Miss Isabella's Dancing Classes for well-brought-up young men?"

He stiffened. She didn't know how close she was to the truth. Then he nodded. "So you think I'm out of date? Let's see." He danced her over to the disc jockey and said, "Play something hot. The lady wants to bounce her booty."

Before Sunny could escape, the Smashing Pumpkins screamed across the ballroom. Seconds later the floor was full. Malone turned into John Travolta and she was sorry she'd ever poked fun at the waltz. If she expected to keep up with him, she'd never do it in the shoes she was wearing.

"What's the matter, Sunny?" he asked over the blare of the music. "Didn't you take your Ginseng this morning?"

She didn't like being goaded. She didn't like being made to look like a fool either. She reached down, slipped off her pumps and moved into a hip-hop step that would have made Puff Daddy weep.

The music, her anger and his challenge drove her. But he matched her, step for step. Before she knew it, he'd drawn her close and was using her body in a thrusting motion that touched her more intimately than her dream lover. From the sidelines, she heard a vague clapping that grew in intensity to the heat of their dance.

She made a move to draw away.

He quickly pulled her back. "What's wrong, Sunny? Can't you keep up with a master?"

"You're no master," she gasped, making one last ineffective attempt to regain control.

"But I'm good," he said with a grin, grinding her hips against him once more.

"Not as good as Lord Sin," she said and jerked away. "Maybe he'd give you some lessons."

The music ended. The crowd applauded wildly and Walt mopped his brow. "Wow, lady!" he said. "Miss Isabella might have been right about turning off the camera. This may be too hot for the viewers in Atlanta."

"Miss Isabella is always right," the birthday girl called out. "Lord Sin knows it but I'm still working on Ryan Malone. Where's my champagne?"

"No champagne," Ryan said, trying to catch his breath. "The doctor said no."

"When the doctor is as old as me, he can tell me what to

do. That was some show you put on, young lady. Where'd you get your training?"

Sunny tried to focus her attention on Isabella. All she wanted was to get off the floor, out of the retirement center and back in her safe, organized life. "Training?" she repeated. "No training. I was an athlete as a kid."

Ryan Malone looked skeptical. "And what sport would feature those moves?"

"It wasn't the sport, it was the people I trained with. They taught me to dance. I was a tumbler," she snapped. "I took gymnastics from third grade until I turned eighteen."

Malone didn't take his eyes off her. They seemed to cut into her, reading her scrambled emotions in spite of her attempt to conceal them. "Why'd you stop?" he asked. "You must have been very good."

"I grew five inches between my seventeenth and eighteenth birthday. Height is fine for basketball but death for gymnasts and ice skaters. Besides, my life went another direction and I became a reporter."

At that moment the lights came back up and one of the young caregivers rolled in a cart carrying a very large cake, with so many candles it looked like a South Georgia sky lit up with stars and fireflies.

An hour later, Walt headed back to the station with the videotape and the notes Sunny had taken so that he could get started on editing the piece. Sunny found herself with Malone rolling Isabella back to her private quarters, listening to the story about how Ryan Malone had bought the cheap little apartment house where she'd been forced to live after her sister died. How he'd moved her into Rainbow House and had supplemented her social security check ever since.

"You're quite a dancer, Miss Isabella," Sunny commented. "Did you ever operate a dancing school?"

"I guess you could say I was a teacher."

"Around here?" Sunny asked as innocently as she could manage.

"Around a lot of places," Malone answered for Isabella. "You haven't lost your touch, sweetheart," he said, touching the elderly woman on the shoulder.

"I guess you've seen Lord Sin perform," Sunny said casually.

Isabella laughed. "Oh, yes. I'm a fan. Sorry I missed the big to-do last night. Always knew he'd go out with a splash. Never expected him to just close up shop and disappear like he did. How'd you convince him to come back, Ryan?"

"Wasn't hard, really. I just told him that this was his last big gesture and he should be here for the final curtain."

"Lord Sin sounds like a compassionate man," Sunny observed. "I'd really like to meet him, Miss Isabella, but he seems to be...shy."

Isabella nodded her head. "Shy? Oh my, yes. Sin is a private person and now that he's retired and living out of the country, even his friends don't see him anymore."

Sunny cut a sharp glance at Malone. "Living out of the country? You mean he isn't in Atlanta?"

"He's still here at the moment," Isabella said with a bittersweet smile. "But I understand he's leaving again soon. Of course, that could change. From what I've heard," she said shrewdly, "he's quite taken by a new lady friend. Really interesting for that to happen now that he's cut his last tie to Atlanta."

"Isabella," Malone interrupted, "you've had a busy day, don't you think I should call someone to help you get comfortable?"

Sunny didn't intend to let him sidetrack her. "You really are a friend of Lord Sin, aren't you, Miss Isabella?"

Her eyes twinkled. "Of course."

"Then tell me where he is."

"Oh, my dear, I'd better not say. He's always been very mysterious," she answered, with a vapid turn of her wrist. "His friends respect that. You might ask Lottie. Now, I'm tired. You two have spent enough time with me. I can manage. Ryan, take this lovely young woman to dinner and show her your talent."

"Showing her my talent is just what I had in mind, Belle." He rolled the silver-haired lady inside, gave her a kiss and turned back to Sunny. "Shall we go?"

"Goodbye, Miss Isabella," Sunny said. "It was a pleasure meeting you. And you be sure you watch WTRU, we'll run your video."

Isabella nodded. "I'll just bet you will."

Sunny turned and left Isabella's apartment. When the door was closed, she demanded, "I know I'm going to regret asking, Malone, but what talent?"

5

EVEN THOUGH SHE'D PROMISED to spend some time with Malone, Sunny had meant public time, covering news events, under the eyes of her constituents. She still wasn't certain how Malone had maneuvered the afternoon so that she stayed at the party while Walt took their video back to the station, but that was what happened. She had to get back to work, but Isabella's parting comment about Malone's talent was ringing in her ears. "All right, Malone," she said as they walked down the corridor. "Confess. What talent?"

In the elevator, Malone hit the button designating the parking deck and the door closed behind them. "I intend to show you, Ms. Clary, tomorrow, privately."

"Whatever plans you have for tomorrow will be a surprise, I'm sure," she said as he opened her door. "But my unemployment won't be part of it. I have to work. Take me back to the station, please."

She didn't think she could handle any more surprises. Then she saw Malone's car and decided she was wrong. Instead of a sports car or a convertible, he was driving a black, American-made sedan. "This is what you drive? Who are you trying to impress, your grandmother?"

"I would if I could, but I don't know my grandmother. I'm an orphan. I drive this car to impress *me*."

An orphan. That stopped her. That wasn't in any of her research. And it was important. After all, she was supposed to e interviewing him. "I'm sorry. I shouldn't have said that. What happened to your family?"

"The only one I know anything about, my mother, died when I was five years old."

"I'm sorry. I lost my mother when I was twelve, but at least I still had my dad. That must have been awful. How did you survive?"

"I just did. A person does what he has to."

"And that's why you're so kind to older women like Isabella, isn't it? You treat her like family. Is she?"

"No. She was just someone being hurt by progress, by my success. I couldn't let that happen."

"What do you mean?" she asked, hearing the caring in his voice, caring that was more than just business.

His voice tightened. "I couldn't displace the people in her building. They were all grand old ladies who deserved better."

"So you bought Rainbow House?"

"Rainbow House has turned out to be a good investment. Now, about what we're doing tomorrow," he began.

"There is no tomorrow for us, Malone. You have to understand. I have a job, one with hours and responsibilities. I go out and tape a story, then I go back to the station where I write the intro, see that the video is edited and hand it over to the news director."

"I have a job, too, Ms. Clary." He moved around to the driver's side of the car and slid in. He indicated his cell phone. "I just carry it around with me. But I forgive your mistake. I understand that you're miffed because I sent Walt back without you. And I'm sorry. I shouldn't have done it."

"Miffed isn't the word for it. And while we're having this discussion, why do you keep calling me Ms. Clary?"

"I'm being professional. If I don't call you Ms. Clary, I

might call you darling and that would definitely not be a
lowed, would it?"

"No, it wouldn't and there's another thing. I resent yo
making plans for me without consulting me. I'm not one o
your...your groupies. You have no reason to take charge o
my life."

Malone looked at her with surprise. He had every reason
She'd socked him in the libido and twisted his insides like n
woman had ever done. She'd even forced him into disclosin
things about himself that he hadn't told anyone. None of hi
bios admitted that he never knew his father and barely re
membered his mother. He'd been very careful to make ce
tain there was no mention of them. And in spite of his excus
to Lottie, there was no logical reason for him to introduc
Sunny to Lord Sin's friends.

He couldn't admit that she was all he could think about; h
was having a hard time accepting the degree of his infatua
tion and he wouldn't let her send him away. But from the se
of her lips when he talked about spending time with her, h
was doing it all wrong. He had to make his proposal mor
professional, win her trust. That's the way he'd reach her
He'd keep reminding her of their business agreement. He'd
promised he'd try to set an interview with Lord Sin if h
could have her.

"You're right. For you, this relationship is business. Fo
me, it's personal. You want your interview. I want you. But
have no right to jeopardize your job. I won't interfere in tha
again. I really do have a job, businesses to run." He flexed hi
fingers on the steering wheel for a moment, then said, "I own
shopping centers, office buildings and I buy and sell real es
tate, but I have people who handle all that. I even have an of
fice and several secretaries that I stay in touch with by phone
Would you like to see my office?"

"Not unless Lord Sin is one of those secretaries."

Ryan laughed. She didn't give up. "I'd never get any work out of my office staff if Lord Sin were one of them. Is there someplace you'd like to go?"

"To the station. You may be able to set your own hours," she said stiffly. "But I have to turn in my story. I won't allow you to interfere with my career. I can't."

"All right. The television station it is."

Sunny leaned back and let out a deep breath. He let her sit quietly for a moment, allowing her to believe that she'd won. After a moment, she relaxed, reached into her purse and pulled out her notepad. "In the meantime, Malone, tell me about your work. How'd you get started?"

God, she was beautiful. In a heartbeat she'd turned her attention back to business. Might as well go along. What he'd done up to now hadn't helped. "Hard work and a small business which I turned into a bigger business which bought more space to rent to more businesses."

"What kind of business?"

That question was a little harder. "I've always been in the people business," he said. "And I'm afraid I've gotten used to people falling all over themselves to please me. I guess I expected the same thing from you. I have an early engagement this evening, but I'm free later. Would you like to meet for a drink to talk about Lord Sin?"

"I would not. I don't want any more talk *about* Sin. I want to talk *to* Sin."

"Maybe we could have some cheesecake and coffee?"

"No, thank you."

"What would you like?" he asked. "You name it."

"To be alone!" she snapped, then added contritely, "With Lord Sin. And you apparently aren't able to do that. So, take me to work, or I'll use that phone to call a cab."

Malone threw up his hands, then turned the car into the heavy Peachtree Street traffic. "Of course. Let's tally the score. I know a birthday party for a senior citizen is tame stuff, Ms. Clary, but I promise to do better. And I didn't say could produce Lord Sin instantly. I just told you I'd introduce you to people who could help."

"Why, Malone?"

"I told you. Because I want...to spend time with you, to get to know you." That wasn't what he wanted to say, but he realized that the words were true. "In order to get to Sin, he has to be convinced that he can trust you." And he realized that those words were true as well, at least the trust part.

"Sin doesn't trust people, but I'm supposed to trust you? Why?"

"Because it benefits us both and because I want you to." *Whoa, Malone, let's not get carried away here. You want to use her dedication to her job to bring a final end to the mystery of Lord Sin. Getting the story can't be too easy or she won't believe it. And if she doesn't believe it, neither will the public. If you work it right, you'll both get what you want.*

"And I don't have any choice, do I? Does Isabella know about our agreement?"

"No. She seems to think you and I are involved—or ought to be."

"I wonder where she got that idea?" Sunny asked.

"Frankly, I thought your dancing with me gave her a pretty good impression of you. Of course, she doesn't know the uncooperative Sunny Clary I know."

That did it. Sunny could be nice. She could even be polite. Her father had made certain of that. He'd been a master at not offending the people he needed to please. Fat lot of good it had done him. And Sunny, after seeing the outcome of his life's efforts, had decided that she'd stand up for herself no matter what.

"I am not uncooperative and I'm not having drinks with you, or cheesecake, or anything else. And furthermore, uness your talent is delivering Lord Sin for my interview, I don't care what it is."

Malone smiled. "You're absolutely right, Ms. Clary. And I realize that you only agreed to allow me to *try* to get you into my bed. So if my attempts have failed, that's my fault—not yours. Still, in the interest of fair trade, you do have to allow me to try. But if introducing you to Lord Sin's friends makes you feel uncomfortable, I'm willing to amend our agreement."

That caught her attention and she turned to him. "How?"

"I'll change the place. I don't have to make love to you in my bed, it can be yours."

THE RECEPTIONIST, whose name Sunny had learned was Melinda, gave Sunny a thumbs-up when she entered the station. "Ted wants to see you. Heck, they all want to see you. By this time next week, the world will want to see you."

"What do you mean?"

Melinda tilted her head toward the monitor on the side wall where the video of the party was playing, not the birthday cake, not Isabella. What Walt had recorded was Sunny and Ryan dancing. There was no missing the heat in their movements or the flash of fire in her eyes. Lord Sin might have toyed with making love to an imaginary woman on his stage but Ryan Malone was doing the same thing with a real woman—her. If this were an educational channel, they'd have fit right into one of those programs about the mating habits of humans. "Oh, my gosh. They're broadcasting the videotape."

"Nah, the video is only on the in-house monitor. They're just drooling."

Sunny looked at the monitor and groaned. Her stern black suit hadn't saved her professional image. She was totally screwed, her credibility ruined. Any chance of proving to

herself or to the public that she was a real reporter was bein[g]
hip-hopped away. She'd be out of a job before the day wa[s]
over. How could she have allowed this to happen? Walt ha[d]
been told to turn off the camera, but blaming him for wha[t]
she was seeing was taking the chicken way out. The reporte[r]
was in charge of getting the story and she'd allowed her at[-]
traction to Ryan Malone to interfere with her job. In th[e]
worst of her trouble in South Georgia, she'd been innocent o[f]
losing her professional edge.

She felt her face flame. Her dance with Ryan was fast an[d]
naughty. Even the black suit didn't come close to concealin[g]
her matching Ryan Malone's seductive moves. She took [a]
deep breath, straightened her shoulders and marched int[o]
the newsroom, straight through the tangle of desks and int[o]
Ted's office. She closed the door and leaned against it.

"I'm sorry, Ted. If you want my resignation, you have it."

He looked up from the copy he was studying and pushe[d]
his half glasses back up his nose, puzzled. "What do yo[u]
mean, your resignation?"

"I behaved in a totally unprofessional manner and I can'[t]
blame the staff for ogling the video. They'll never respect m[e]
again."

Ted looked confused. "Ogling? Respect? I don't know
what you're talking about."

"Oh? Then you haven't been looking at your own monitor."

He swung his chair around, saw the television screen on
the side wall and came to his feet. "What the...?" He stood,
looking for a long minute until the dance ended and the camera cut to Isabella and the birthday cake with a hundred candles. At the sight of the hundred-year-old, Ted's frown
turned into a broad smile and he looked back at Sunny.
"That's good stuff, lady. You've already set this town on its
ear with last night's video. Malone is Atlanta's most eligible

bachelor. This just made you one of the beautiful people. At the rate you're going, you'll be the hottest reporter in Atlanta. I may have to give you a raise."

"I don't want to be hot, Ted. I want to be respected, and how can I expect respect from the city of Atlanta when I'm making the news instead of reporting it?"

Ted walked around the desk and put his hands on Sunny's shoulders. "Hey, you were invited to a party. So you had a little too much fun. We'll edit that out. I'm sorry if the video embarrasses you, but you're going to have to develop a thicker skin. Otherwise, this town will chew you up and spit you out. Now, sit down and let's talk."

Sunny swallowed hard. Ted was right. She'd gotten caught up in her flirtation with Ryan Malone and she'd learned a real lesson. She wasn't nearly as tough as she'd thought. Slowly, she walked over to the desk and sat in the hot seat in front of Ted's desk. Before he could say anything, there was a knock on the door and a sheepish Walt came in. "Sunny," he said, "I'm sorry. This was all my fault. You told me to stop videoing but you two were so good I couldn't resist. Then I put it on the monitor. But believe me, nobody intended to embarrass you."

Ted put his hands together, his index fingers pointing as if he were having a heavenly consultation. "You know, Walt, you may be right. It's not often a person does something that spontaneous that makes you want to say, *yes!* You may not think this kind of exposure is good for your image, Sunny, but since we're building your television persona, maybe your image should include more of a sense of humor. We get enough straight news reporting. I think I like this—not—" he cut his eyes to Walt "—that I think a cameraman should make a habit of disregarding the instructions of the reporter." He nodded his head. "Yes, this is good."

Sunny groaned. She was doomed. "You call that good? I

call it tabloid journalism. Where's the truth in a story like that?"

"The truth," Ted said. "Everybody looking at that story will see it differently. The older generation will see the joy of life. The middle-aged will see a brighter future and the younger group will think that WTRU is cool. You will have touched them all. Maybe we ought to use the piece. It's that good news I was talking about."

"I shouldn't have danced with Malone, Ted—granted. But *you* shouldn't show it to an audience. They have a right to expect serious journalism—not a latter-day Hugh Hefner doing a bump and grind with me."

"Our viewers have a right to feel good about the news, Sunny, and you're giving them that."

"I don't want to be the good news anything. I want to be a cutting-edge reporter who exposes the thieves. Atlanta has enough crime and corruption to let me have a piece of it. When do I get my chance?"

"Tonight. I'm sending you and Walt to cover the mayor's Inner City Awards Banquet."

"All right!" Walt said dryly and left the office. "Last year one of those little con artists tried to pick my pocket."

Sunny groaned. "Reformed juvenile delinquents? That's your idea of an assignment covering crime and corruption?"

Ted shook his head. "No, but that's where you'll meet the people at City Hall you need to know. Around here the police have to trust you before they'll accept you on the crime beat and the way to make them trust you is to make them like you. What about it?"

"The crime beat? You'll assign me to the crime beat?"

"If you'll let me show your dancing with the most eligible bachelor in Atlanta, I'll let you have a shot at our political leaders."

She could have argued, but the truth was she'd brought

this on herself. Even if it wasn't what she wanted, it made Ted happy. And she had to defer to his judgment. "Deal! I'll make those kids look like Harvard graduates."

Ted let out a relieved sigh. "Good!"

Sunny headed out the door. "I'd better get to work." She stopped and turned back. "I'm curious, Ted. Would you happen to know anything about Ryan Malone's special talents?"

That brought a stunned look to Ted Fields's face. "No. Not unless it's about making money."

"I don't think that's it." Sunny shook her head. "Never mind. I don't want to know anything about the man that isn't newsworthy. Just tell me he isn't paying for this banquet tonight."

"I've been told the funds for the dinner came from the Mayor's discretionary fund."

"Good!" she said, waved goodbye and left the office.

"But Malone is getting an award," Ted called out in a loud whisper that got lost in the closing of his office door. He picked up the phone and punched in several numbers. "Too bad," he said to himself. "I don't think she heard me. But I do like the way this is going."

RYAN DECIDED TO WORK the rest of the afternoon at home. Once there, he punched in Lottie's number and waited. She picked it up instantly, as she always did. He wasn't ready to admit it to her, but it was becoming apparent that she was right about Sunny Clary. The reporter was becoming an obsession. How else could he explain his behavior this afternoon?

"Hello, Sin."

"Why weren't you at Isabella's party?"

"I intended to get there but I was shopping and it took longer than I thought."

"Shopping?"

"I bought Isabella a birthday present and a present for you, too."

Missing the party of an old friend wasn't like Lottie. "I'm sure she wondered where you were. And it isn't my birthday."

"I called her and explained that I was going on a mission of mercy. And since you've hidden everything else about your life, you can make your birthday any date you want."

"Lottie, I'm almost afraid to ask. What kind of gift were you looking for?"

"You know, that's the funny part. I knew what I wanted. It should have been simple. But everything changes, doesn't it?"

"What changes, Lottie? What wasn't simple anymore?"

"Shopping. Do you know how hard it is to find those blow-up dolls now?"

Ryan rubbed his forehead. Sometimes Lottie's games weren't games at all. He couldn't understand what she was up to this time, but he'd never hurt her feelings. She was a shield between his past and the present and the only person he'd ever completely trusted.

"Ryan? Are you there? Don't get your britches in a wad. I didn't go to the party because I didn't want to watch you self-destruct. Then I turned on the television and there you were, doing just that in front of the world."

"They've already run the story?"

"About five minutes ago. Even I didn't know you could dance with a real partner."

"Lottie, it might surprise you to know that there are any number of things I can do that you don't know about."

"Name *one*. No, never mind. I don't want to know. I don't want to see you going down in flames because of stupidity. I didn't expect you to make the television screen your boudoir. Are you trying to tell the world *you're* Lord Sin?"

Ryan let out a deep sigh. "You're right, Lottie. I can't afford to do anything that will mess up my image for the next two weeks. It's just that Sunny Clary is the first itch I haven't been able to scratch and she's driving me wild."

"My advice is for you to buy yourself some calamine lotion and find a less dangerous lady. How about the woman you're taking to that banquet tonight?"

"Damn! I'd forgotten. I'm taking the hospital's PR officer, Anne Kelley."

"I thought you weren't going out with her anymore."

"I'm not. She's just a friend."

"Well, if you're looking to get that itch scratched, a friend might be the one to do it."

But she wasn't. From the moment Ryan spotted Sunny and her cameraman entering the Commerce Club later that evening, he knew Anne couldn't do it. Neither would calamine lotion. He needed a rain forest to cool his heat.

He'd known Sunny Clary would cover the banquet; he'd suggested it. Seeing him with another woman was supposed to rattle her. But he was the one off balance. He felt as if he were cheating on her—an emotion he'd never experienced before.

Tonight she was wearing a simple pale green dress with a matching jacket. The skirt was short, showing off her impossibly long legs to perfection. Her hair was loose about her face, soft, caught only with a jeweled clasp at the back of her neck. Restraining that mass of hair was like trying to keep ribbons from flying in the wind. Running his fingers through it was an image that kept hitting him every time he saw her.

"The new reporter for WTRU," Anne said. "She's lovely, isn't she? And there's an energy about her that's contagious. I'm hoping they'll send her to cover the dedication."

"Energy? I suppose, though I don't understand it," he admitted. But he felt it, every little tear in the structured fabric of his world widening with its force.

"She has charisma. All the best TV people do. But it's more than that," Anne said. "The energy she gives off is dynamic. Can't you feel it?"

"Yeah, there's something explosive about her. I'm just not certain about the fallout that comes with the explosion."

Anne looked at him and smiled sadly. "So, it's like that, is it?"

He took a drink from his wineglass and swallowed slowly, watching Sunny laughing at something the police chief was saying. "Like what?"

"The great Ryan Malone has finally fallen for a redhead who is on the fast track to the top. And maybe she's too independent to appreciate the Malone treatment. Figures."

"What makes you say that?" Ryan asked, wondering how she'd seen so clearly what he'd been trying to cover up with bargains, bets and smoke screens.

"We've been friends for what? Two years?" Anne said. "I've seen you look at a lot of women, but you never looked at any of them like you're looking at Sunny Clary."

"She makes you notice her."

"Yeah, I saw her at the Valentine's Day fund-raiser. She's a beautiful woman."

"No," Ryan argued. "Beauty isn't the issue. It's the way she goes after what she wants."

Anne had a quizzical look. "And what does she want?"

"The truth. For starters, she's determined to expose the identity of Lord Sin."

"Well, I wouldn't want to be that guy. I'll bet she won't give up until she does."

Ryan groaned silently. If his plan didn't work, he could

end up being that subject if he weren't careful. "Let's find our table before the mayor gets started."

"Sorry, Ryan. I'm supposed to be the information officer. I sent out fact sheets but Sunny hasn't yet learned who is who. I think I'd better go do my job."

"By the way, Anne, Ms. Clary doesn't know about my part in the hospital yet."

Anne nodded her head. "I won't say anything. I haven't told anyone who didn't have to know. But she's a reporter, and if she's as good as I think she is, she'll find out."

"GOOD EVENING, I'm Anne Kelley, the public information officer for the evening. I believe you know Ryan Malone?"

Sunny managed to respond. "Yes, it seems Mr. Malone has an uncanny talent for showing up at every interesting event in the city."

"That he does," Anne agreed. "You'll learn he's very involved in Atlanta."

A few minutes later, Anne escorted Sunny and Walt to the front of the room where she introduced Sunny to the people responsible for the event.

Sunny forced herself to concentrate on her assignment instead of the man across the room who was continually undressing her with his eyes. Ted must have known Ryan would be here. Why hadn't he warned her? Because he'd fallen under the spell of Malone's charm, that's why. Well, in the future she'd be ready. Anne Kelley was right. It was Sunny's job to cover the news and Malone was a big part of it. She wouldn't be caught unprepared again. She'd wear Teflon underwear and carry a shield if need be to erect some kind of barrier between the heat of her desire and the source of it. And she'd remember that Malone was her ticket to Lord Sin.

Over the din of children's excitement and with Anne's

help, Sunny was able to get the necessary head shots and quotes. She didn't have to look around, she knew exactly where Ryan was sitting.

"I saw your piece on the retirement home, Ms. Clary," Anne was saying.

"Please, call me Sunny. And I hope you don't think that's the way I usually get a story. But Mr. Malone is a hard man to put off when he makes up his mind."

"Yes, I've had some experience with his persistence. In spite of the press, he's managed to keep the full extent of his charity work secret. He likes it that way."

Sunny cut a sharp look at the dark-haired woman who was her information source for the evening. "I...I understand that Mr. Malone has a great many...friends. He seems very—likable."

"If you're asking...yes, I like him. But friends is all we are," Anne confessed. "Not that I wouldn't have liked more, but Ryan always seemed driven in such a way that there was no room for a woman in his life—at least not permanently. I always wondered who'd change that."

"I don't know what you mean," Sunny said. "Mr. Malone's personal life appears to be something of a mystery. I spent all afternoon with him and all I learned was that he was an orphan who didn't know his father."

Anne looked surprised. "I've known Ryan for two years and that's more than I ever learned about his past. It was obvious he didn't want to talk about it and I respected that. I never learned much about his present either, unless it involved helping people."

Sunny felt a jolt of guilt. Malone was nice, genuinely nice and no matter how much she tried to pretend otherwise, she liked him.

As they moved from table to table, Anne identified the political and business leaders present but it was the children

who caught Sunny's interest. They were so full of awe to begin with, gradually relaxing when they understood that they
were with people just like them.

One little boy with a big wide smile and a gaping hole
where his front teeth ought to be caught Sunny's attention.
"What's your name?" she asked, holding out her microphone.

The boy ducked his head and she had to lean down to
hear. "My name's Octavius Henry Lawson."

"And what did you do to earn an invitation to the banquet?"

"I cleaned the trash out of the vacant lot, all by myself."

"That sounds like a big job," Sunny said. "How long did it
take you?"

With a worried frown, Octavius Henry Lawson looked up
at the elderly woman sitting with him. "A long time."

"All summer," she said. "Some of that junk, and the rats,
was bigger'n he wuz, but he didn't give up. Now," she said
with pride, "we got us a little park with swings, all because
of my grandboy."

"You must be very proud of him," Sunny said, then added
for the benefit of her television audience, "as we all are.
These youngsters have all given their time to make our city a
better place. Tonight, they are being rewarded." She lowered
her microphone and said, "That's enough for now, Walt,
let's take a break until the speeches start. Thank you, Anne.
You've been very helpful." She almost escaped as she turned
and headed toward the outer hallway of the elegant Commerce Club where the event was being hosted.

"Ms. Clary!"

Almost. Ryan Malone was bearing down on them. She let
out a sigh and stopped. "Yes?" She turned back to face him
and regretted that she hadn't kept walking.

"How do you like the club?"

"The club? The building is very nice." She was puzzled. Surely he hadn't stopped her to discuss the facilities.

"I'm glad you like it," he said, staring at her as if she'd left her clothes back at the station. Walt, the rat, had ducked into the hallway and disappeared, leaving her alone with Malone in the entranceway. "Is there something you need from me, Mr. Malone?"

"Oh, yes, ma'am. You know it. We've pretty well covered what we both need and want. I just thought tonight might move us closer. Are you impressed? I'm giving you another good-news story. Don't I deserve something in return?"

He was smiling at her, daring her to admit he was making progress. She was no coward. So far he'd pursued and all she'd done was back away. Maybe it was time she stopped. She put her hands on her hips. "You're right, Malone, why don't you just give me a great big kiss right here in front of everyone and get it over with?"

He looked startled for a moment, then grinned, raising one wicked eyebrow. "I don't think so," he said, and took her by the hand. "Come with me."

"Now wait a minute. I wasn't serious. I can't leave the building." Sunny tried to shut down the aggravating little voice that kept saying, you brought this on yourself. At the same time she realized that she wasn't really fighting him. It had been that way from the start. Her words said no but her body refused to listen.

Seconds later, he pulled out a key and opened a room off the corridor marked, Sales and Marketing. He pulled her inside and, before she could protest, he lowered his mouth to hers and kissed her.

She hadn't known a man could kiss like that. She didn't know she could return such a kiss. Maybe it was because they were in the dark and she couldn't see him. Maybe it was because she was so ready that she was on the verge of exploding. *Oh, Pop, I hope you're right about following your instinct.* She kissed him back.

Ryan felt the change immediately. She was pushing with her palms, but then the push gentled and she sighed and leaned against him, all soft and clinging. He heard warning bells ringing that said this wasn't a woman out for easy sex, but there was no way he could stop. The furious churning abated and he felt something strangely gentle. And finally, his fingers left her shoulders and captured her hair. Even the red strands, now caught between his fingers, felt hot.

He groaned. Or maybe the sound came from her, and pulled back. Resting his chin against her forehead, he tried to still his breathing. She didn't speak and neither did he. Then came a knock at the door, followed by "Sunny?"

"Walt!" she said, and jerked away. "Yes?"

"They're about to start the speeches," he said. "You want me to video the mayor?"

"Yes. Go on in, Walt. I'll just finish up what I'm doing and join you."

"Sure thing," he said. "And don't forget to turn *on* the light on your way out."

Sunny heard the sound of his laughter, then only the sound of her breathing. "Mr. Malone," she finally said.

"I wish you'd call me Ryan."

"I wish I'd called a cop. Turn on the light, please."

She didn't want a light, didn't want to see the aftermath of the heat wave she'd just experienced but she had to face the world and she didn't have time to find a ladies' room.

The soft light of a lamp suddenly pierced the darkness. Ryan Malone stood behind the desk, staring at her incredulously. "I'm not going to apologize for kissing you, Sunny. I've wanted to do that again since that first time—a real kiss, not just a quick touching of the lips. If I was too rough, I'm sorry. I'm not usually like that."

Malone seemed to be as confused about what was happen
ing as she was. And this time, she'd responded to his kiss
Maybe she ought to be blunt and tell him the truth, even if i
cost her a meeting with Lord Sin. She'd started out tellin
herself that she'd go along with his preposterous propositio
if it meant getting the story, but somewhere along the wa
that was changing. To what, she wasn't sure. She finall
raised her gaze and looked at him.

Atlanta's most eligible bachelor's hair was mussed. Ha
she done that? And his tie was crooked. She grinned. "Yo
look like you've been making out. If my face looks anythin
like yours, you might have well have kissed me back there i
the banquet hall where everyone could see."

"That can still be arranged," he said.

"I don't think so. It'll end up on the nine o'clock news an
my career will end up in the toilet. Is that what you want?"

This time he didn't smile. "The last thing I'd want to do i
interfere with your work, Sunny. Maybe we'll save the kiss
until after the awards ceremony." There was a seriousnes
about him that wasn't there before. "There's a bathroom
right through that door," he said, looking at a narrow doo
by an antique table. "You'll find anything you need," h
said.

She hesitated, wanting nothing more than to start the eve
ning over. But she couldn't let him know how profoundly
she'd been affected. "Thanks," she said, opened the doo
and switched on the light. She was facing a mirror over a
porcelain sink. The mirror reflected a woman she'd neve
seen before. Her hair was flying wildly, as if she'd just wak
ened. Her lips were swollen and red. She looked like she'
just been made love to and no amount of repair was going t
change that. Still, she had to try. Splashing cold water on he
face removed some of the flush. A drawer revealed a comb

with which she managed to restore some sort of order to her hair.

Finally, satisfied that she'd done the best she could, she returned to the office to find it empty. She didn't know whether to be pleased or insulted that Malone would disappear without an explanation. Quickly she slipped into the hall and back into the banquet room where the mayor was saying, "Octavius Henry Lawson, for his hard work in cleaning up his neighborhood, is being rewarded with two weeks at summer camp in the mountains of North Georgia."

Octavius, now over his shyness, bounced forward, took the trophy from the mayor and shook the hand of the man standing next to him. Ryan Malone. The boy started off the platform, then stopped and turned back. Ryan said something and the child took a flying leap, landed in Ryan's arms and hugged his neck. When Ryan let him down, he gave the boy a thumbs-up and watched proudly as he danced down the steps and into his grandmother's arms.

A grandmother, that was another thing Sunny hadn't had. Both sets of grandparents had died before she was born. Then she'd lost her mother. But her father had been enough. At least to the best of his ability, he'd tried. Then he'd been sent to jail. Until then, he'd believed that hard work and living right brought a man rewards. Losing that trust had almost destroyed him. His despair had driven Sunny to search out dishonesty. She'd thought that would make everything better. But when she'd tried to tell her father about the corruption in Martinsville, he'd warned her, "Sometimes, people kill the messenger because they can't deal with the message." He'd been right. She'd lost her job and the truth had been concealed.

"You okay?" Walt asked.

"I'm working on it," she answered more sharply than she intended. "Is this guy for real? Retirement homes. Children. Grandmothers?"

"The children and the old folks seem to believe in him. Don't you?"

"I don't know." She knew Walt was asking about more than the story, but she didn't have an answer.

One by one, each child accepted a trophy, shook Malone's hand and exchanged a thumbs-up with him. Sunny felt her anger melt away as she watched. Ryan Malone, the lover, had turned into Ryan Malone, proud parent of twenty-six kids. At least she'd had her dad, even if he hadn't quite known how to show her he cared. Ryan had no one. So he'd created his own family.

Finally, the mayor presented the last award, then picked up a plaque and said, "Now, it is my distinct pleasure to announce the final award, recognition for a great humanitarian, the man who made it possible for all these boys and girls to go to summer camp, Ryan Malone."

The applause was deafening. In moments, every person in the room was standing.

Ryan looked embarrassed. His hair was still mussed and his tie was still crooked, but it didn't matter. He was as elegant as he was generous. After shaking hands with the other officials on the platform and with the mayor, he said humbly, "Thank you, but I'm not the winner here. I'm not the one to be recognized. The winners are these kids, kids from broken families, often without a place to live, who deserve better than we give them. Children deserve hope and respect. I know how they feel. I've been there. I've been fortunate enough to be able to give back and so long as I can, I will."

Ryan's speech rang true, and Sunny knew he was sincere. She motioned to Walt and they quickly left the building. All the way back to the station she expected Walt to say something, ask questions. He didn't, until they pulled into the parking lot. "What are you going to do about him?"

"I don't have a clue. I never met anyone like him. All I know is that he's too much for me."

Walt chuckled. "I doubt that. He's made it clear that he's interested in you, Sunny. I think it's going to be great fun finding out what he does next."

6

HER PHONE RANG at midnight.

The voice was low and seductive. "Hello, Sunny. Why did you run away?"

"Malone, don't you ever give up?"

"Not when I find something I want."

Sunny sat up in bed and pulled the covers to her chin. "To-night—the kiss—was a mistake," she spoke softly into the telephone. "You know it."

"Probably, but even if I wanted to, I couldn't stay away from you. And I don't think you want me to."

"It's late, Malone. What do you want?"

"You, here with me. I want to kiss you again. Close your eyes, Sunny. Imagine it."

"I'm not good at imagining. I much prefer reality."

"I like reality, too. Especially the reality of you kissing me back."

"It was just a kiss, Malone."

"Maybe. But you can't fake a response like that. I know you felt the same thing I did."

"I was just surprised."

"Don't lie to me, Sunny. The truth, remember."

He was right. How could she lie to him if she was commit-ted to exposing lies and corruption? "You're right. I was shocked but I...your kiss was awesome."

"And so was yours. I want to see you, Sunny. Just say the

word and the next sound you hear will be me, knocking on your door."

"No, please don't. Ryan, I can't do this. I have a job, a job that's important to me. I'm not wealthy like you. Earning my own way is important, so is sticking to my plan. You're messing up my head and I can't let you do that." There was desperation in her voice, fear even. She couldn't think rationally. What if he really came over? She was barely in control. Desire flared at nothing more than the sound of his voice. She couldn't resist him any more than Lord Sin. At least Sin was a fantasy.

There was a long silence. "All right, Sunny. I won't push you. I told you I want you but when we make love, I want you to want it, too. I'll wait."

"Good night, Ryan."

"Good night, Sunny. Oh, one more thing. I've arranged for you to talk to Lottie tomorrow. Are you still interested?"

She took a quick breath. She'd given up on a meeting with Lord Sin. Apparently he was willing to keep to his bargain. But it was her decision. Was she willing to keep to her part of the bargain? "Not tomorrow," she finally answered. "I need a day to do some research and get my schedule together. Could you postpone it until the next day?"

"Coward!" he whispered.

"It's just that I don't think I can see you again so soon, Ryan. And that's the truth."

"All right, Friday it is. She's invited you to tea. Shall I stop by the station for you about four?"

"Friday, at four," she agreed.

"Good night again," he whispered. "By the way, stretch knit sheets aren't bad. Don't know why I never tried them before."

"You're sleeping on stretch knit sheets?"

"I'm not sleeping much, but I'm trying."

Sunny ran her fingers over her smooth cotton sheets and smiled. "You're kidding," she said.

"I never kid. And just in case you're interested, I'm trying out your idea of nightwear as well."

"My nightwear?"

"Yeah, cologne and a smile."

SUNNY CALLED HER FATHER every Sunday. Calling him on Friday morning was an abrupt departure from her normal routine. "What's wrong, Sunny girl?" he asked.

"Nothing really. I just wanted to hear your voice."

"Uh-huh. So, let me hear you telling me why you needed to hear mine. Is it the job?"

"The job's great, Pop."

"Your apartment? Maybe you'd be better off in one of those condos. I'm a little worried about your being by yourself."

"No, I love my garage apartment. The people who live in the big house in front are in Florida so I have plenty of privacy. Everyone in town doesn't know what I'm doing. I like that."

Well, her statement sounded good. It should be the truth. But according to Melinda, if the telephone calls and e-mail were any indication, her life with Ryan Malone was quickly becoming front-page news.

"Then what's wrong?"

She'd never told her father that the politicians she'd wanted to expose were associates of the man who'd owned the construction company where he'd worked. Even though he'd been blamed for their corruption, the inferior materials they'd used, he'd gotten over being bitter. She never had. No one had believed her father and she figured out right away that no one would believe her. So Sunny had made it her goal to go after the criminals, changing her college major to

ournalism to give herself the credentials and a forum to expose their wrongdoings. But her boss had put a gag on her.
She'd failed.

Then her father had decided to go into the ministry, believing that all that he'd suffered was leading him to serve
others. She'd known that she couldn't put him in the spotlight again.

But this was a different kind of dilemma.

"I've met someone. Someone I don't quite know how to
handle, Pop. I guess I'm just scared."

"This isn't like you, Sunny. You've only been there two
weeks. Isn't this kinda sudden?"

"It isn't at all like me. I only met him a couple of days ago.
But he's like a freight train coming at me and I can't seem to
get off the tracks."

"Never known you to be scared before. Guess I can take it
to mean that you're not physically afraid of him."

"No. I'm afraid of me."

"You like him?"

"Like? I don't really know. He likes me, at least he likes
my...attitude."

"So, what's wrong with him?"

"Nothing. But my instinct tells me that there's something...not quite right. He's very attractive, wealthy, goodhearted and he's interested in—me? That scares me."

"And I always told you to go with your instincts, didn't I?
Tell you what. I'd planned to come up and check out your
new living quarters," her father said, suddenly serious. "I
think I'll just drive on up after church on Sunday. Think I
could meet him?"

"Yes," she said. "I'd like that."

Her father had tried to be there for Sunny after her mother
died. And they'd spent time together, time arranged more
often by Sunny than her dad. He never seemed unduly upset

at her escapades. Part of it, she knew, was that he was just too tired to argue. But he also simply wanted her to enjoy life. Her yellow treehouse might have raised a few eyebrows in their small town, but he'd pronounced it the mark of a happy place. Gymnastics instead of ballet seemed a good idea. He worked along beside her on building a Habitat for Humanity house, teaching her how to use a hammer and nails and a saw. When she'd decided to become an actress, he'd pronounced it to be a fine career. By the time she entered college, she'd grown used to his weary smile and automatic approval. He hadn't been there when she'd changed her college major from theater to journalism but he'd known he was the reason she'd set her sights on exposing corruption and he'd warned her to be careful. She was glad he was coming. Byron Clary was a man whose judgment had been impaired once. Neither he nor Sunny would ever make that mistake again.

She wanted her father to use his judgment on Ryan Malone.

"I SHOULD HAVE KNOWN!" It was later in the morning and Sunny was in the room affectionately called the station's morgue. She'd just pulled up the computer file of Ryan Malone's real estate holdings and discovered that the Commerce Club belonged to him.

"What's up?" Ted Fields, foam cup half full of coffee in his hand, took the seat at the computer next to Sunny.

"Just doing a little research on Ryan Malone," she said, exiting the file and leaning back in her chair.

"Good piece you did on that awards banquet last night. The man never ceases to amaze me."

"You know you misled me about Malone, Ted," she claimed with affected anger.

"No, you asked me if he was paying for the dinner and I said no."

"Yeah, that's the only thing he didn't pay for. Even the building belongs to Ryan Malone."

"I knew about the building, but I honestly didn't know that he'd financed all those kids attending summer camp. He keeps a lot of his philanthropy to himself. Understand your public information officer for the evening was Anne Kelley. She's a good contact for you. How did you get along with her?"

"I like her fine." *Except that she's one of Ryan's ex-girlfriends.*

"Walt said you had a little trouble with Malone. He seems concerned. Frankly, so am I. Maybe you'd better drop this business about interviewing him."

"Interviewing *him* isn't my first choice, Ted. I'm working on unmasking Lord Sin. Malone is the way I get to Sin, and he's also my consolation prize if I don't find Sin."

"Forget Lord Sin for now. I have a new assignment for you. Ever covered a celebrity golf tournament?"

"Not in February. Isn't it a bit cold?"

"Not for these guys. It's a local thing, not covered by the networks. But we tape the highlights. I'm sending Walt with you."

"He ought to be happy. At least this is a sporting event. When do we go?"

"Tomorrow morning."

"Oh!"

"What's wrong? Don't tell me you don't have anything to wear."

"No, it isn't that, I just had something planned. But that's all right, I'll call and change my appointment from tomorrow to today. May I leave about four?"

"Sure, in fact, go whenever you like. Once you do the two stories I assigned to you, you're free."

"They're done. Thanks." Sunny sprang to her feet and headed to her desk, her mind whirling a mile a minute. She'd just call Lottie and change having tea at her place to something less personal, like going out for lunch. An hour later she'd given up. Ms. Lottie Lamour was a ghost. She'd have to call Ryan. If Lottie was a ghost, Ryan was a spirit. Yes, he had phone numbers but the voices on the end of those numbers were pleasant, perky and firm. Each took her number and promised to get it to Mr. Malone as quickly as possible.

It was two o'clock when Sunny's phone finally rang. "Sunny Clary. May I help you?"

"It's me," Malone said. He didn't even have to identify himself. The sound of his voice did it for her, immediately firing her nerve endings.

"About having tea with Lottie, do you think we could make it today? I'm on assignment tomorrow."

"Pick you up at four," he said.

ALL HIS GOOD INTENTIONS went out the window when Ryan opened his car door to help Sunny Clary inside. He'd seen her story on the children, the tenderness and dignity with which she'd told it. It touched him that she understood how he felt about these kids. After a night of swearing that he'd do this last thing, then back off, he took one look at her and knew that he was only fooling himself. He was attracted to her, but he was learning that he liked her goodness, too. "Hello, Sunshine."

Sunny grimaced as she sat down. "Don't call me that. My mother called me Sunshine."

"I'm sorry. I didn't mean to bring up bad thoughts."

"No bad thoughts about my mother," Sunny said. "She was an angel. It's just that nobody ever called me Sunshine before, except her."

"What happened to her, or would you rather not talk bout it?"

"Brain cancer. Headaches. Tumor. Surgery. Malignant. he died within six months. I was twelve."

"That's tough." Ryan said. He knew what it was to watch our mother die. He took Sunny's hand. He couldn't help ut notice the smudges beneath her eyes. She wasn't sleeping either. That should have bothered him, but it was oddly reassuring because his sunglasses were hiding the same telltale signs on his own face. Now he'd given her more cause or concern.

The day was dark. A battleship-gray sky gave birth to an cy wind whistling down Peachtree, gathering up leaves and pieces of paper and flinging them angrily about. Sunny was dressed in a camel-colored wool coat that fell midway to her calves, and camel-colored leather gloves. Sensible brown pumps and opaque hose covered all he could see of her legs. The only cheery addition to the somberness of her dress was a bright tan-and-yellow scarf around her neck. With her briefcase under her arm, she pulled the ends of the scarf loser with one hand while the other caught her auburn hair nd held it close to her head as he closed the door behind her nd moved to the driver's side. "I hope it wasn't too much of n imposition on Ms. Lamour."

"Hard to tell," he admitted. "Lottie is a woman with a mind of her own and sometimes I can't fathom her at all."

"She doesn't want to see me."

"No, quite the opposite. She is delighted. She likes you." And that disturbed him.

"Where does Ms. Lamour live?" Sunny asked, bringing him back to the present. "I've been studying a city map."

"She lives in Vinings in a house that survived the Civil War. At least some of it did. After the war, the owner rebuilt t but it's hard to tell the old from the new. By the way, I think you might want to drop the 'Ms.' Lottie likes to think of herself as a modern woman, but she's really very old-fashioned."

"Do you see a lot of her?" Sunny asked curiously.

"No, but I did work with her in the transfer of the club to the Arts Council and in arranging the program for the fund-raiser. She's fiercely loyal to Sin and she'll peck your eyes out if you threaten him."

"Must be nice to have someone so protective," Sunny observed.

"They were together a long time. They trust each other."

"Sometimes loyalty and trust are an illusion." She thought of her dad and the man he'd worked for. "You think you can count on someone only to find out they're using you. I hate that. I really hate that."

Ryan cut his gaze to Sunny. She was serious. Who in hell had made her so suspicious? He thought about her mother's name for her, Sunshine, and he had a sudden need to make her smile. "The governor's mansion is on your right. We're on West Paces Ferry Road where the real estate is worth a few bucks."

"Do you live out here?"

"Me? No. I have an apartment at the top of the Malone Building in Buckhead and an apartment downtown."

"And Lord Sin? Where does he live?"

Ryan swallowed a smile. She thought she'd just run that into the middle of their conversation. Smart idea. Sunny didn't know it yet, but she was going to be told eventually. Given his recent state of mental confusion, it might have worked. "Don't know. Sorry. Maybe Lottie will share that information with you."

"But you don't think so, do you?"

"I never predict what Lottie will do. We're crossing the

Chattahoochee River, heading into Vinings. This is a pretty historic area if you're interested."

Interested? Oh, yes. She was interested, but not in anything historical. If it wasn't in the present, it had better be research for a story she was working on. Looking at Ryan was definitely not research, though she did have an undeniable urge to touch his upper lip with hers. "I'm interested in Lord Sin," she said crisply, sure that he could see the blush that flamed her cheeks. "And I'd appreciate it if you'd stick to business."

"Look," he finally said, "why don't we try to forget that I kissed you last night? Just sign it off to the fact that you're an appealing woman and I behaved badly. I don't usually do that. I apologize. And, if you'll let me, I'd like to get to know you better."

"So, you find me appealing. You were quite open in telling me that you want my body. You said that if I let you *try* to talk me into your bed, you would help me reach Lord Sin. I agreed to let you try. You just caught me by surprise last night. I was the one overreacting. But I'm ready for you now. So, have at it."

That brought another smile to Ryan's lips. In between bouts of self-recrimination he'd been smiling a lot lately. "You think I'm not going to? Move over a little closer and I'll show you my best shot."

"Pay attention to your driving or you'll be showing it to the judge."

He reached the intersection of the two narrow streets in the middle of Vinings and turned into the drive of a white clapboard frame house with gingerbread trim along the roof of the porch. "Not your fault that you don't know how to appreciate real talent," he said, smiling.

"And what talent is that?"

"Obviously, my kisses aren't up to par. You already told me I needed to take lessons from Lord Sin. Maybe I'll arrange to talk to him, collect a few tips before he leaves," he said and turned off the engine.

Lottie was on the porch waiting for her guests. "Good to see you, *Mr.* Malone, and you, too, Miss Clary, is it?" Today she was dressed in a pleated wool skirt and matching sweater. On a chain around her neck she wore an antique sun-shaped pendant with what appeared to be Chinese writing.

"Please, just call me Sunny."

Lottie nodded. "Come in out of this wind. I know that February must be the worst month of the year. When Sin was young, he used to call it Uglywary."

"So Sin—"

"Not yet," Lottie stopped her. "Let's visit for a while first."

Sunny swallowed her impatience and, with Ryan at her elbow, followed the statuesque beauty into a house straight out of the forties. It could have been designed for Jane Russell or Joan Crawford. White furniture and drapes, with accent fringed pillows of gold and green. Pale gold carpet and tables made from blond wood.

In the center of a bay window overlooking a small garden, Lottie had laid out a white lace-covered table for tea. Silver tea service, delicate cups with lavender designs and two silver trays filled with scones dripping with golden jelly and little sandwiches covered with cucumbers and garnished with tiny apostrophes of pimento.

"Oh my, I feel like I'm on a movie set. This is beautiful, Ms. Lottie. Did you decorate it yourself?"

"I did. I made all the drapes and covered the pillows."

"I'm very impressed. You must have been a designer before you retired."

Lottie smiled and sat gracefully on the couch. "You might say that. I've always had an eye for color and fabrics. Take her coat and hang it in the closet, Ryan, and close your mouth. This is woman talk. Do you sew, Sunny?"

Sunny allowed Ryan to help her out of the coat and take it away, pretending not to notice the caress his fingers made along her chin. "No, I don't know a thing about sewing."

"Doesn't surprise me. Girls don't get taught the way I was. From the time I could stand on a stool and reach the counter my aunt made certain that I knew how to cook, sew and play the piano. She never lived to see how I'd use those talents. But I'd like to think she would have approved. What about you?"

"My mother died when I was twelve," Sunny said. "My father tried to teach me, but he didn't know much about those things. Instead, to be close to him, I learned to keep books, saw, nail and paint. If you need something added or repaired, I'm a whiz."

Lottie looked impressed with her skills. "I'm thinking now that's a good thing to know. I've been fortunate in having male friends who would trade a little muscle for a good meal."

"That's what I'd hoped to talk to you about, Miss Lottie."

Lottie looked surprised. "Being a handyman?"

Sunny laughed. "No. Male friends. I know you're a friend of Lord Sin's. I wonder if you'd tell me about him."

Lottie stood and started over to the tea table. "I don't usually talk about Sin. But maybe I will, today. At least I'll talk about the club—if you like. Let's have tea first. I've made blackberry. I hope you like it."

Ryan followed dutifully. "I hope you have something a little stronger, Lottie," he said.

"If you'll put that handle back on the drawer in the kitchen you might find some wine in the cabinet."

The laugh Ryan let out said what he thought about repair

work as he left the room. "You expect me to be one of these handymen?"

"No," Lottie said sharply. "I expect you to go away and let me chat with your lady."

"I'm not his lady," Sunny said as soon as Ryan was out of hearing distance. "I don't know why everyone keeps assuming that."

"I do. I saw the two of you dancing on TV. My screen is still scorched."

Sunny grimaced. "I saw it, too. Pretty awful, wasn't it. I wish the station hadn't aired the tape. I want the viewers to take me seriously."

"Never apologize for enjoying life." Lottie poured the pale lavender-colored tea into the china cup and handed it to Sunny. "It's better with cream and sugar," she said and plopped a lump of sugar into the cup. "You add the cream."

When both cups were dressed to Lottie's satisfaction, she took a dainty sip, looked straight at Sunny and asked, "You're falling a little bit in love with Ryan, aren't you?"

Sunny chewed on her lip thoughtfully before answering. "I hope not. I've only known the man for a few days."

"That's long enough. If you belong together, forget all this nonsense about Lord Sin. You won't regret it."

"Oh, Miss Lottie, I'm having a hard time separating Sin from Malone."

She laughed. "I can understand that. They're both very appealing. Never married, but I had two men in my life. Loved them both. I keep hoping I'll meet another but I guess I'm getting too old to think about a man. There just aren't any good ones left."

"My father is a good man," Sunny said, then wished she hadn't when she saw Lottie's interest.

"I'd like to meet him. Think he'd go for an ex-stripper?"

Sunny gulped. She didn't know how to answer. In fact, she

had no idea what her father would think about Lottie. She'd never seen him with any woman except her mother.

"That's what I thought. Have a pastry."

Sunny took one of the dripping confections and, juggling it and the tea, took a bite. "Oh, my goodness. This melts in your mouth. I can't believe either of those men let you get away."

"They didn't. Sent one packing. The other? Well, maybe I'll tell you about the other sometime."

"Tell me about The Palace Of Sin," Sunny said, finishing off her pastry and helping herself to a sandwich. "How do you know so much about it?"

"Worked there for forty years."

Sunny couldn't control her shock. "Really?"

"Well, it wasn't known as The Palace Of Sin when I started there. It was a vaudeville house called The Ho Ho Palace."

"Ho Ho?"

"Believe it or not, it belonged to a man who was half Chinese. His name was Ho. Never figured out whether it was his first or his last and, eventually, they both became the same. I worked as a dancer in the chorus until Ho sold the place and went back to San Francisco. The next owner turned it into a burlesque house and I just kept on dancing until I got too old. You look like a dancer yourself."

"I danced some, yes. But I was a gymnast, until I grew too tall."

"Why did you decide to become a reporter?"

Sunny helped herself to another sandwich and thought about her answer. "Because of my father."

"Oh, he was a reporter, too?"

Sunny shook her head. "No, my father was an office manager, a bookkeeper for a man who was in the building business. He's a Baptist minister now."

Lottie gave Sunny a measured look. "You responsible for the change?"

"Not entirely, though I'm sure I contributed."

"Are you two close?"

"Not always, but we're closer now."

"I like that. A child should be close to her parents. They ought to protect each other."

"We do, or at least he's very protective of me. I'm afraid I failed in my attempts to look after him. But I tried." She tossed her head and took a bite of her sandwich. "As a matter of fact, he's coming in on Sunday for a visit."

Lottie held out the platter of sandwiches. "Thought you said he was a preacher. Isn't Sunday his big day?"

"It's a very small church. They only have services twice a month. He came to the ministry late in life and he was assigned a church nobody else wanted."

"Why did he become a minister?" Lottie asked.

Sunny took a deep breath and let it out. If she was going to convince Lottie to help her reach Lord Sin, she had to gain her acceptance. "I told you my father was an accountant. He was sent to prison for falsifying records and taking bribes—something he didn't do, Miss Lottie. He vowed he would never handle money again."

"So he couldn't handle money." Lottie laughed. "Well, he found a profession where he sure won't have to, didn't he? What happened to the real crooks?"

"Some of them are still around, but his boss drowned in a sailing accident while my father was in jail."

"I'd say the good Lord took care of the situation right well, didn't he? How're you doing in there, Ryan? It's awfully quiet."

"I'm looking for a screwdriver, Miss Lottie."

"In the drawer by the *back* door." She looked at Sunny and smiled.

"About the club, Miss Lottie, when did Lord Sin come into the picture?"

She looked out the window for a moment, then answered. "He was sixteen, too young to even be there when he started. Lied about his age, he did."

"Sin started dancing when he was sixteen?"

"Oh, no, not on the stage. He just played around with it, with the girls. They loved him. His job was to clean up the place, act as a gofer. Just did odd jobs while he went to school. But he had the talent. Always had the talent. He had his moves, even then, and he was smart enough to use the skills God gave him to get where he wanted to go and determined enough not to let anything stop him."

"And where did he want to go?" Sunny asked, softly, almost afraid to stop Lottie's reminiscences, for she understood now that the woman was reliving a part of her past as well.

"I don't think even he knows yet. But maybe he's closer than he was."

That wasn't the question Sunny had wanted answered. She'd hoped for a location, not a state of mind. But Lottie was being much more reachable than she'd been that night at The Palace Of Sin. And Sunny was beginning to like her.

A howl from the kitchen, followed by a clatter, did what Sunny's questions hadn't, brought Lottie to her feet and ended the trip down memory lane. "What have you done now, you rascal?"

In the kitchen they found a chagrined Ryan holding a handle in one hand and a screwdriver in the other. On the floor was the drawer and all the silverware.

"It slipped," he said, grimly.

Lottie laughed. "You've spent too much time learning to make money. You should have practiced using a screwdriver more."

"Well, I have other talents."

Sunny wanted to laugh at his ineptness. He'd been listening at the door and must have heard her tell Lottie about her father. She held out her hand. "Give me the screwdriver," Sunny said, picking up the drawer and taking the handle from Ryan. In no time she had the handle reattached and was replacing the scattered utensils.

Lottie shook her head and gave a tsk, tsk, tsk. "I think you'd better forget having wine, Ryan, and have some tea instead. Sunny has to get home in one piece. Her father's coming for a visit on Sunday, or did you already know that?"

"No. I didn't know that. Leave it to you, Lottie," he said. "You could ferret information out of a secret agent."

"Did that once," she said as she led them back into the living room. "Didn't know what to do with it when I got it. The nice young man from the FBI had a hard time making his report. Finally said he'd better avoid dancers in the future."

"I'll bet," Ryan commented dryly, following the two women into the parlor. "Did you get a commendation from J. Edgar Hoover?"

"No, but the guy from the Bureau didn't miss one of my performances for the next two months. I was afraid I was going to have to adopt him, too."

"What happened to him?" Sunny asked, taking a seat on the satin divan. She'd heard Lottie's "too" but didn't want to stop the flow of information by asking about it.

"He met Isabella and switched loyalties immediately. Have some tea, Ryan," Lottie said and sat across from Sunny. "Now, where were we?"

"We were talking about your FBI agent and Isabella. Would that be the same Isabella who had the birthday party at Rainbow House?"

"The one and only," Lottie admitted. "The silly thing is still vain. I was good, but she was always better. That's beause she was the most erotic of the dancers. Guess that's why they made her Sin's teacher. She broke in all the new dancers but Sin went far beyond all the others. He was the answer to every woman's dreams."

"Isabella taught Lord Sin?"

Lottie nodded. "She taught him how to dance."

"I think we'd better be going," Ryan said, suddenly standing behind Lottie. He leaned down and gave Lottie a quick kiss on her cheek. "Thanks for the tea."

Lottie gave him a flick of her hand. "You didn't drink any yet. What's wrong with you? You asked me to give Sunny some information on Lord Sin and that's what I'm doing. She's not ready to go yet. Either go for a walk or be quiet."

"Lottie," he said in a warning voice. "Lottie, I don't think Lord Sin would appreciate your being quite so frank."

"Why? I'm talking about the club, not about him. But if I were to decide to, I could tell this young woman a thing or two. Maybe I will. Sin needs to learn that maybe he's not always right. Besides, I like Sunny Clary. Any girl who has an ex-con for a papa and still cares about him is okay in my book."

"Isabella may have taught Lord Sin to dance," Sunny said quickly, in an attempt to cut off any questions from Ryan, "but I'll bet you taught him other things that were equally important."

"I like to think I did."

"I found him very—interesting," Sunny said wistfully. "I wish I could have seen him perform more than once."

Lottie smiled. "You know, I may be able to help you there. I think I have a tape of one of his rehearsals."

"Lottie!" Ryan started toward the door. "Let's go, Sunny, before Lottie gets in big trouble with Lord Sin. You do want your interview, don't you? He might decide not to give it to you."

"Yes, of course I still want the interview." Sunny stood, puzzled at the sudden underlying tension in the room. "I'm sorry, Miss Lottie. I didn't intend to get you into any trouble."

"You didn't get me into anything," she said, looking resigned as she stood. "Fetch her coat, Ryan." She turned back to Sunny. "I've enjoyed this afternoon and I like you. I didn't intend to, but I do. Sometimes I think we keep too many secrets." With her back to Ryan she leaned down and picked up a tape from beneath a table. "If you and your father aren't too busy, I'd love to meet him," she said and stuck it into Sunny's briefcase.

Sunny returned her smile and walked to the door where Ryan was waiting. "I think he'd like that very much," Sunny said. "Perhaps we can have dinner."

Lottie slapped her knee. "Of course. Ryan will cook for us. Won't you, Ryan?"

Ryan looked cross but he managed a weak smile. "Perhaps."

"You cook?" Sunny asked, trying not to respond to his frown.

"I told him to show you his talents," Lottie said. "This is only one of them. He's also good at—"

"Goodbye, Lottie." Ryan gave her a quick kiss, opened the door and ushered Sunny out before Lottie could finish her sentence.

"Dare I ask about your other talents?" Sunny asked as Ryan closed his car door.

"If I were you, I wouldn't."

"Why are you so angry, Ryan?"

"I'm not angry. I just didn't expect the two of you to become best friends. Normally, Lottie is like a clam. Today, she turns into Lord Sin's personal publicity woman." He took a deep breath, then looked at Sunny. "I'm sorry. I don't know why I reacted like that. I promised you I'd help you get to people close to Lord Sin, that they'd be the ones to determine whether or not they'd intercede with him on your behalf. I just didn't expect it to really work."

"It hasn't—yet," Sunny said.

"But it might. Sunny?"

She turned to look at him as he'd hoped. Their eyes met and held. She was incredibly sexy, her hair slightly mussed from the wind, her lips parted as if in surprise. "You know I want to kiss you," he said.

"No. You don't. Let's go, Malone."

"Not yet." He reached out and caught her cheek, holding it gently. Her skin grew warm, warmer, as if the imprints of his fingers were being permanently etched on her face. "Don't look so stricken, Sunny. I won't hurt you."

"But you could," she whispered. "Everyone says—"

"Everyone says what I want them to. Don't you understand?"

"And what do you want me to say about you, Malone?"

She was afraid of him but she didn't turn away. He could almost feel the wild, crazy desire that surged through him transfer to her. "I want you to say that you want me, Sunny Clary."

"No," she protested. "I won't. So you can stop coming at me."

"But you do," he insisted and he kissed her, a slow, deep kiss that branded her as surely as the fingertips still holding her face. He let go with one hand and pulled her closer, sliding her legs over his knees and slipping his hand beneath her coat to turn her toward him. He expected her to freeze. She didn't. Instead she threaded one arm around his neck. Suddenly her coat was open and her breasts were pressed against him and hungry, white-hot passion raced through him. As his fingers found her breasts, she groaned and pushed against him. Then suddenly there was an intrusion, an insistent noise at the window.

Reluctantly, Ryan pulled away and turned, to come nose-to-nose with Lottie peering through the foggy window.

Sunny groaned and scooted to the other side, pulling her coat around her like a shroud.

Lottie knocked again and motioned for him to lower the window.

"What do you want?"

She smiled, looked over at a mortified Sunny and handed him a box wrapped in white paper with a red bow. "It's your gift. Remember? The one I bought for you. And from the looks of things, I believe you've generated enough steam to blow it up."

7

"You going to stay puffed up like a frog all the way home?" Ryan asked, feeling like a kid caught in the act at lover's lane. He still had an erection that showed no signs of abating.

"I am not puffed up like a frog!"

"Then what else do you call it?"

"I'm embarrassed," she confessed. "What must Lottie think about me?"

"The last person you need to worry about is Lottie. I believe she's showing definite signs of sexual deprivation. In fact, the way she's been acting, it's your father you should be concerned about."

"My father? What does that mean?"

"Never mind. Forget what I said. It's just that this kind of frustration is something I'm not used to. Look, we're adults. I know you want me. You know I want to make love to you. What are we going to do about it?"

"Nothing! Absolutely nothing," Sunny snapped. "I'm not going to be one of your two-week women."

"Two-week women? What does that mean?"

"One of the first things I heard about Ryan Malone was that you were Atlanta's most eligible bachelor, that you were seen with every beautiful woman in town for two weeks and then you moved on. Do you deny it?"

"Of course I do...I..." But she was right. He hadn't played elusive on purpose, he just hadn't felt strongly enough about

any of them to take a chance on the relationship turning s
rious. Until now.

"See, you can't deny your reputation. So there won't
any us. And I'd appreciate it if you'd stop talking about it.
fact, the deal's off. Forget about helping me with Lord Si
I'll...I'll find him by myself."

Ryan let out a deep sigh. Just what he didn't want. "N
you won't."

"How do you know? I'm a reporter, remember?"

He didn't argue because he couldn't be sure. One thing
did know. Sunny Clary was no two-week woman. "Loo
Sunny, we got started off on the wrong foot. If we'd met an
where other than Lord Sin's performance, we'd have gotte
to know each other and..."

"We'd never have met, Malone. I'm not in your leagu
You're the penthouse suite. I'm the garage apartment."

"I wasn't always. There was a time I didn't even have
place to live."

There was a long silence. He'd confessed something he
never told another soul. A slash of late afternoon sunlight fe
across Sunny's face. It fired the red in her hair and fed th
connection between them. Except this time, it wasn't just d
sire he felt, it was understanding.

RYAN DROPPED SUNNY at the television station where sh
spent the next two hours returning calls from people wit
news tips and typing up the information for Ted. Then sh
drove herself back to her apartment.

She didn't know how she felt about what had happene
She just knew that it had changed. The heated encounte
she'd just had with Ryan Malone was still as powerful as be
fore, but she'd gotten a glimpse of the man behind the fir
Homeless? Alone? And he wanted them to be friends? Cou
friendship survive such desire?

Climbing the steps to her apartment she felt her briefcase bump her leg. It reminded her of the videotape Lottie had given her. Watching Lord Sin after making out with Ryan Malone would be overwhelming. The body could only take so much stimulation. She refused to allow herself to play it until she'd eaten dinner, showered and was ready for bed. Finally, doing her best to close Malone out of her mind, she slipped the tape into the VCR, snapped off the light and started the machine.

The screen was black for the first few feet but the music was there, a kind of new-age fairy music that suggested flutes and pipes in the distance. Then, as the sound grew louder, a faint light appeared in the distance, like a firefly, growing closer and closer. Then the music slowed and the movement of the light stopped. The tiny flame flared for a moment, then turned into a sunburst of light.

Lord Sin suddenly appeared. A luminescent body, like the core of the flame, a spirit that transcended time and space. Every line of his powerful body was outlined in a shimmering, golden glow. He was covered by the same kind of translucent material he'd worn at the fund-raiser. It became an outer skin in the light. His long golden hair was caught in some invisible wind and tousled wildly. Then, as he swayed back and forth, the light changed from golden to a silver as soft as moonlight.

He played to the camera as he had to the women in his audience, moving close enough so that, just for a second, she could see the brilliant blue of his eyes peering out from the mask that covered his face. Then he pulled back, seeking the shadows as he spoke. His voice was the same low, sensual whisper, his words a mental caress. "Come closer, darling. Close your eyes and touch my body with yours. I feel your desire. We're only strangers in the real world. In your fantasies we've met before. Tonight we'll make love again. Touch

me. Let me touch you. Let me give you what you want. Yo
will never be alone again. Let me show you what it means t
have a man desire you, make love to you."

His movements were so fluid and so smooth that h
seemed to move from the television screen to the bedroom. I
was unbelievable how he stimulated the mind so that th
viewer saw what he wanted her to see. And every move wa
designed to suggest two bodies entwined.

"Feel my mouth on yours, drawing the sweet taste of yo
into mine. Feel my hands touching you, caressing your nip
ples. Now my lips leave yours and take those nipples int
my mouth, hot, moist, demanding. I'm asking you to war
me, to let me give you the dreams you need. Do you war
me? Are you ready to take me inside you?"

Incredibly, Sunny felt her own body sing. Oh, yes. She wa
ready. The moist heat between her legs said yes, even thoug
in some faraway place, her mind still questioned. Not thre
hours ago she was in lust for Ryan Malone. Now this. Wa
she turning into some sex-starved woman who craved ever
man she met?

"Soon, my darling," he whispered. "Soon, you'll welcom
me into your bed."

She swallowed hard. There was more, but for now, sh
needed sleep, not more stimulation, not being forced to ac
knowledge her desire. She was already flying on the raw
edge of emotion. Tomorrow was the golf tournament an
she couldn't let her incredulous attraction to either Lord Si
or Ryan Malone interfere with the future she could have.

Between the two of them, they'd kindled a fire that neve
completely disappeared. Instead it remained banked unti
something, or someone, stimulated it. She punched up he
pillow and pulled up the cover. How naive she'd been suc
a short time ago. She'd fallen in love in college, hot swee
love that lasted until she'd seen him with another girl. The

she'd had a casual fling with her editor until she'd surprised him by investigating the city's great plans to bring new industry to Martinsville. Until she'd found out about padded expense accounts and payoffs to the same men who'd profited from her father's alleged crimes. Then her story had been killed, for the good of the town, he'd said. It was time for her to grow up. When she threatened to tell the truth anyway, he'd told her she'd only hurt her father. To protect him in his new church, she'd gone quietly.

A blessing in disguise, that escapade had been, for she'd packed up her belongings and headed for Atlanta. The major television stations hadn't given her the time of day, thanks to the man she'd thought she cared for. But Ted Fields remembered her freelance work for the station during the flood and he'd listened. Ted had believed her. He'd even urged her to talk to the officials in the governor's office. But she wasn't sure she was ready to do that yet. Her father had told the truth and nobody had believed him. If she took on the officials back in Martinsville all that would come up again. She couldn't do that to him. But she'd resolved never to be silenced again.

RYAN'S FIRST CALL that night was to Lottie. "Why'd you do it, Lottie?"

"Do what?"

"Give her that tape. I thought it had been destroyed."

"How'd you know? Did she tell you?"

"No, I saw you in the mirror."

She sounded stricken. "I don't know, Ryan. I should have destroyed it, but it was like my personal photograph album of you. I couldn't let it go. Besides, I like her and I think you like her, too. I've decided that telling the truth isn't such a bad idea."

"But the truth has to be my truth," he said, his voice rising.

"If we give her the story, she has to tell the world Lord Sin is a bastard named Jack Ivy who lives on the Riviera, not Ryan Malone."

"Hey, calm down. It was your idea, remember? I wasn't sure you were serious. I thought you were using 'finding Lord Sin' to stay close to her. Maybe you'd better make up your mind what you really want."

Lottie was right. The offer had started as a kind of foolish jest. He'd try to get her to Sin if she'd come to his bed. He hadn't seen any further than the red curls on his pillow. Now the deal was off and he was still toying with giving her the story, at least the one he wanted told. What he couldn't honestly say was why.

"Ryan, I think it's time you stopped backing away from women because you lost your mother. I don't think it's burying Lord Sin that's got you worried. I think you're just scared she won't understand."

"You're right. She wouldn't. I suppose that makes it all right that she's more interested in Sin than she is in me."

Lottie laughed. "You sound jealous. You are Sin, babe, and if you aren't careful, sooner or later, she's going to figure it out. No matter what you do."

"I don't know, Lottie. Sometimes I'm not sure who I am. Jack Ivy was a loser. Ryan Malone didn't exist until he became a wealthy citizen; then it was his money that drew people—people who wanted to benefit from that money. Now Sin is about to disappear. Where does that leave me?"

"Jack was smart enough to create Sin and the women loved Sin for the way he made them feel. Then Jack created Ryan Malone. Think of all the people Ryan's helped. They love him for his generous heart. And you and I know all those people are one and the same. They're all you and you've built something special. Just like what you're building with Sunny. Don't dismiss that."

"When did you get so smart about relationships, Lottie?"

"I've always been smart about other people's lives, Ryan. It's just my own that I messed up."

"Everyone knew Ho was a rascal, Lottie. You could never see that."

"I knew it," she admitted, "I just loved him anyway. I knew better than to go with him but I always thought he'd come back. Take my word for it, settling for what *might* have been makes for a lonely life. Wonder how Sunny's father deals with that."

"Lottie, don't you dare. I think you're going through mid-life crisis. The man's a preacher."

"He is now," she said with a chuckle he didn't trust. "What are you going to cook for us?"

"I never said I was going to cook."

"But you are, aren't you? Because you want to see her again."

"You're right. I'll cook, but Lottie, you leave her father alone. I don't want you showing off."

"Ah, all right. Just seems silly to look a gift horse in the mouth without at least examining his—teeth."

Two hours later Ryan was at Harry's, the local gourmet food market, where he filled his basket with greens and fruit and a pork tenderloin.

From what he knew about Sunny, she didn't do anything halfway. He'd bet Sunny's father was the same way. He wondered what kind of man produced Sunny Clary. As he stashed his groceries in the car, he knew he was going to find out. He only hoped Lottie didn't have the same agenda.

WHEN RYAN CALLED, Sunny was wide-eyed and edgy, and she realized that it wasn't just Sin's tape that made her restless, she'd been waiting for Ryan's call.

He went straight to the point. "I'm sorry I was such an...ass," he said.

"So am I," she said, ignoring the possibility that he was apologizing for what happened in the car. "The meeting was your idea. Lottie and I were getting along fine. What happened?"

The silence told her he was considering his answer. "I think I was surprised," he finally said. "Lottie has never been quite so open with anyone before, not even with me."

"You mean you were jealous?"

He laughed dryly. "You could say that."

That surprised Sunny. "But you were trusting the people close to Lord Sin to size me up. Apparently, Lottie decided I was okay. Isn't that what you intended?"

"Yes. And Lottie is hardly ever wrong. So, from now on, I'm a friend. As you said, our deal is off. And I'm following Lottie's orders. I'm cooking for you and your father and Lottie on Sunday night. That is, unless you think he won't be comfortable with an ex-showgirl."

"My father isn't uncomfortable with anyone."

"Then I'll expect you about six." He hesitated. His voice dropping lower. "I wish it was tomorrow. Tomorrow I'll have to be with shallow people who think they're important when they're not. I'd rather spend it with you."

In his bed, she thought, then felt her heart race. The pounding of her pulse was her constant reaction to the thought of Ryan Malone. If only she could think of him as something other than a potential lover. But it was all tied in together. His kisses and the way they made her feel. Watching him with the children at the banquet and feeling an absurd ache that she couldn't explain. Odd that she was thinking about what a good father he'd make. And a good husband. Even so, she refused to believe he was serious about being interested in her.

It had started with Lord Sin who'd released all these unfamiliar feelings when he'd reached out to her on stage and, later, in her dreams. But it was Malone who was here in her thoughts, making her crazy.

"And what would we do," she finally asked, "if we spent an ordinary, real day together? As friends?"

"We'd go to the mountains, poke around in old antique shops, maybe stop by a mine and shovel up a ruby or two. Do you like to fish?"

"Tried it a few times," she admitted, "but I decided I like sitting by the water and reading a good book better than catching fish. Are you a fisherman?"

"Never done any," he admitted. "But I think I'd like the peaceful feeling it seems to give. I have a rough little cabin up in the mountains built over two streams. Bought it from a man who built it himself. In the spring, when the mountain laurel blooms, I go up by myself, open the windows and just listen."

"You go alone?"

"Why do you sound so skeptical?" he asked.

"I don't know. I guess I just think of you as a tycoon and a..." she couldn't say lover, though that's what she meant and she thought he knew that "...philanthropist who could afford a mansion. Why a rough little cabin?"

He waited a moment before answering. "Because it's honest. It isn't expensive and fine. No pretense. It's just what it is."

"So what are you doing tomorrow?" she asked, drawing back from the appealing intimacy he was creating. Ryan Malone confused her in ways she didn't understand.

"Tomorrow I'm playing in a charity golf tournament."

That news jerked Sunny back to reality. Ted's "good news" again, no doubt. Was the rest of her television future going to revolve around Ryan Malone? "Are you any good?" she finally asked.

"As good as a few thousand dollars of lessons can buy. But skill isn't the point here. The match was organized to raise money for Doctor's Hospital's new children's program."

"If skill doesn't matter, why didn't you forget about the lessons and give the money to the fund?"

"The lessons were a long time ago," Ryan confessed. "Before I found out what I wanted to do with my money. At a time when I thought appearance was as important as substance. But I found out I like playing. It's relaxing. What do you do for fun, Sunny Clary?"

She liked this conversation. It was normal, not sensual. Particularly tonight, after the feel of Ryan's hands on her breasts and watching the tape of Lord Sin, she could appreciate normal. It was too bad that normal and sensual couldn't be combined in one man. But she knew enough of the world to know that was unlikely. "I run, and I like the theater."

"So do I. I have season tickets to all the shows in town," Ryan said.

"Of course you do. But what I meant was that I like being involved in the theater. I'm not very good but I was a volunteer in our little troop before I came here. Mostly I worked with the children."

"You should sign up to help out at the Arts Council. They could really use you now that they're going to have a new theater."

"Maybe I will."

"Lord Sin will be signing the papers next week and the committees will swing into action."

"Will it be a public signing, with the press present?" she asked, her pulse racing at the thought of seeing her phantom lover in person.

"I doubt that. He'll be represented by counsel."

"You'd think, now that it's all over, he wouldn't object to being seen in person."

"He might if he trusted the press."

"Why? If he's never been interviewed, how could he distrust them?"

Ryan almost told her. He almost said that it was the press who hounded his mother until she couldn't face life anymore. But he couldn't do it—not yet. "What did you think of his video?"

Sunny gasped. "You knew I had it?"

"I saw Lottie give it to you, in the mirror near the door. You watched it?"

"The beginning," she admitted. "He is awesome. I don't know how he learned to reach out to women like he does."

"He practiced. After all, he's been doing it since he was sixteen."

"I still find it hard to believe that he started as a sixteen-year-old," Sunny said. "What happened to his parents?"

"I don't think he ever knew them," Ryan said.

"That's very sad. At least I had a father."

In the ensuing silence, Sunny inadvertently yawned, then repeated the yawn, loud enough that even Ryan heard her.

"Well, it's getting late," Ryan said reluctantly, "I'd better let you get some sleep. Maybe I'll call you later tomorrow. What do you say we give ourselves another chance?" he asked with what she knew was a smile on his face.

"Another chance at what?"

"At deciding how we feel about each other. My offer is still good. No conditions. I think you ought to know, I've slept with other women but I've never brought another woman to my bed."

All he had to do was mention his bed and she was wide awake. Forget peaceful tranquillity by the lake. She almost told him that if he'd bring the blanket, she'd bring lunch and a condom. "After that make-out session in Lottie's driveway, I'm not sure I believe anything you say any more than I'd believe Lord Sin."

"Oh, but Lord Sin's a fantasy. I'm real. And I want to see you before Sunday."

She knew that she wanted to see him before Sunday, as well. "You will," she said, glad that he couldn't see the smile on her face. "I'll be at the tournament. I'm covering it for the station. I don't suppose you called Ted again?"

"Nope. He did this on his own. Think he's throwing us together?"

"I think he's up to something. Of course you'd know better than I about ulterior motives."

"Me? I'm wounded. And I was lying here thinking that tomorrow would be a good time for you to ask me some questions. I mean you still want that interview, in case you don't find Sin, right?"

Interview Malone? That had been part of their original deal. While they searched for Lord Sin, she could interview him along the way. She mulled that thought over in her mind. Could he be trusted? What would she ask him if she could be certain he'd tell her the truth? He seemed to be a man who fiercely protected his privacy and she was a reporter. Oil and water, destined to travel separate paths. He'd made a big deal out of getting her into his bed, but she figured that was just his standard line and no matter how much she wanted him, she had no intention of falling for that come-on. With his looks and money, he could have anyone he wanted—probably had.

And she was an inexperienced nobody. As a trainee at WTRU whatever name she had up to now was coupled with his, not the kind of reputation she wanted. Once he dropped her, she'd lose her audience.

"What about it, will you share my lunch box tomorrow?" ie asked.

Lunch with Ryan? She'd like an hour of uninterrupted ime with the tycoon in a public place. Public would be good. *rivate would turn into kisses and touching and wanting. "I an't be sure. I'm covering the tournament, at least Walt is. *his is all new to me. I doubt they all stop and go to lunch at ie same time."

"No, they'll give us a box lunch to eat along the course. Let Valt keep filming and if something happens you can do a oice-over later."

"And how will I be able to eat this lunch with you?"

"That's simple. I'll arrange for you to follow my partner ind me. He's famous enough that WTRU will be happy."

She laughed. "Yeah, and who is your partner?"

"I imagine you've heard of Joe Andrews, the Atlanta Braves baseball pitcher."

"Sure, and the tournament is going to let me be his hadow? I don't think so. I'm low man on the totem pole as ar as the press is concerned."

"They will if I want you," Ryan said simply. "And I've been very honest about that. I do. Now get some rest. I'll see ou tomorrow."

ON THE WAY TO THE FIRST TEE, Walt had a curious grin plas-ered on his face. "This is going to be very interesting," he *aid.

Sunny followed Walt, surprised at the number of people ilready gathered. She'd been told that a charity event didn't isually draw a crowd. "What do you mean, interesting?"

"Well, the piece on the Mayor's Awards brought a lot of elephone calls, primarily about Sunny Clary and Ryan Ma-one. One woman even asked if there was something going on between you two."

"I hope you told them no" was Sunny's caustic reply.

"I would have but my mama told me I should never tel lie so I suggested that Melinda tell them if they wanted find out for themselves they should check you out at the g tournament."

"You did what? There's nothing going on, Walt," she gued, wishing her argument was true.

"Uh-huh, then how come we get the prime photog pher's spot today? Besides, look at this crowd. Why else a they here? Think of all the money you're raising for charit not to mention our ratings."

He came to a stop and waited for Sunny to notice the pla ers standing on the green.

"Joe Andrews and, surprise, Ryan Malone. This is no a cident, is it? Didn't you see the reporters at the check-stand? If looks could kill, we'd be pushing up the daisies. B cause of you and Malone, we get preferred treatment and tl hospital makes more bucks."

She blushed, averting her gaze from Ryan's casual no "Well, I did talk to Mr. Malone. He asked me to have lun with him."

"And in order to do that, we had to be in his group. O lady, I think I may like being your man. How do you fe about football?"

"Does Malone play football, too?"

Walt laughed, then touched his finger to his lips. Tl group was about to tee off. Ryan went first. Sunny watche him position his feet, take a few test swings, then pull ba his club and hit the ball. It might have been on target. On the appreciative sigh of the crowd gave her a clue since sl was caught up in watching Malone. Dressed in casual nav trousers and a yellow polo shirt that stretched tight again his chest when he swung, he looked magnificent.

"What about that?" Walt said. "He could have been a professional."

Sunny jerked her gaze from the man and shaded her eyes to search the course. His ball lay about halfway between where he was standing and the flag. At that point Andrews hit his ball which soared through the air, landing within two feet of Ryan's.

"You're probably looking at the two best golfers in the match," Walt said in a low voice. "And that's just where they'd want to be."

The crowd surged forward, carrying her and Walt along with them. Malone didn't keep up with Andrews, but he didn't do badly. By lunchtime, Sunny was hot and her legs were aching. She really had to find a city park with a jogging trail.

When a golf cart appeared at the edge of the woods, Ryan motioned for Sunny to come with him. "Go on," Walt urged. "I'll see you down the green."

With what appeared to be half of Atlanta watching, Sunny walked across the green and crawled in. "Could you have made it more obvious?" she asked crossly. "I mean we're the only ones in a cart. Why'd you do it?"

"So we'd have time to eat and talk between this hole and the next one. The interview—remember?" He turned, left the fans behind and drove through the wooded area to a special path for carts between the fairways where they couldn't be seen.

This morning she was dressed in a pale blue silk T-shirt, navy slacks and blazer. Her hair had been pulled back and threaded through the back of an Atlanta Braves baseball cap. She looked professional and appealing.

"Where are we going?"

"To someplace more private."

"I was afraid of that," she said, her voice practically̲ moan.

He stopped the cart and turned to her. "I didn't thi̲ you'd want me to kiss you in public."

Just as he leaned forward, his lips headed straight ̲ Sunny's, Sunny let out a cry and jerked back, flapping ̲ shirt like clothes on a wash line in the wind. Then she w̲ out of the cart, dancing around. "Help me, Malone!"

"Help you do what?" He followed her, confused, helpl̲ to do whatever she was asking.

"There's something stinging me, in my shirt. Get it ou̲ With that, she flipped the shirt up again, exposing her la̲ covered breasts to him and the world.

Sunny Clary might be fearless in the face of danger, but̲ insect sting was sending her into hysterics. Ryan swallow̲ his amazement and looked for the bug. A red spot about t̲ size of a dime was obvious. It had already begun to swe̲ But there was no sign of any creature. Tentatively, he pull̲ the lacy bra aside, reminding himself that he was on ̲ emergency medical mission.

"There it is," he announced, taking the wing of a tiny y̲ low-and-black honeybee and lifting it from its mortal resti̲ place in the valley of Sunny's breasts. It wasn't spring y̲ The flowers were budding but there was no reason for a ho̲ eybee to have been anywhere around their golf cart. But t̲ evidence was right in front of them.

A peal of laughter and a clicking sound broke the silen̲ announcing that they were not alone. Sunny let go of h̲ shirt, whirled around and headed into the woods. Ry̲ started after her, stopped and looked back in time to see̲ man with a camera disappearing in the woods on the oth̲ side of the trail. Ryan's indecision cost him. Sunny was go̲ and so was the mystery man. "Damn!" Malone frowne̲ climbed in and started the golf cart again. This could be a ̲

ster. He had his hands all over her breasts when the pic-
ure was taken. Who would believe that he'd been searching
r a bee? Anybody seeing the pictures would only see his
ngers inside Sunny's bra. What in hell would this do to
eir already shaky, very public, relationship? Sunny would
robably never speak to him again. That thought stopped
im. For the past five years he'd protected his reputation
ealously and suddenly it wasn't his reputation he was wor-
ring about, it was Sunny's.

He left the cart in the woods and caught up with Sunny
nd Walt walking down the green. Sunny refused to look at
im. "You know if that picture gets out, I'm probably going
be the laughingstock of the television industry," she said
a tight voice. "This little bit could end my career as a seri-
us journalist."

"I'm sorry, Sunny," Ryan said. "I wouldn't want to be re-
ponsible for ruining anyone—ever."

Walt kept conspicuously quiet.

"You didn't do it, Malone," she said. "You couldn't know
at I'm scared of little flying creatures. Who was the man
ith the camera?"

"I don't know, but I intend to find out. Now, we're coming
p on the next hole. Put a smile on your face and let's eat our
unch. If you want to physically harm me later, you can do it.
ut I'd say to hell with whoever he was. I intend to let the
orld see my interest in you."

"That's easy for you." Sunny said. "You didn't expose
our—body to that world."

Walt cleared his throat. "Sorry. Just forget I'm here."

"Don't worry," Malone said, ignoring Walt. "If I need to
efend your honor, I'm prepared." He held up the hapless
nsect. "I have the excuse for my actions." The honeybee
vent into the pocket of his shirt and he handed Sunny a box.
'Have something to eat."

She managed a weak nod in return, snatched the box fro
his hand and opened it. "Here, Walt," she said, dividing th
sandwich inside and handing him half. "But watch out f
bees."

Ryan smiled again. Sunny did that to him. She w
spunky, this woman he was drawn to in spite of the potenti
consequences. Joan of Arc had nothing on her. If someon
tied her to the stake, she'd stand there and spit in their fac

He watched her take a big bite of meat and bread an
chew it lustily, licking a smear of mayonnaise from her u
per lip. The sight of her tongue was as erotic as her breas
had been. If they hadn't been in public view, he'd hav
kissed her again. He had to tighten his resolve not to do
anyway. The idea that some zealous fan could cause h
harm was more than he could stand. He wouldn't allow th
shots to hurt Sunny. Because of him, Sunny was in the publ
eye, not professionally but on a much more personal leve
And he had to protect her.

It was Sunny's reputation that he was concerned abou
not his. So what if his past would be dragged out and exam
ined minutely. It simply meant that he had to make certai
Sin was gone and that there was no way anyone could t
Ryan Malone to the stripper he'd been.

Sunny polished off the sandwich and was munching on
pack of chips. She looked worried but in control. Her gree
eyes sparkled and he couldn't tell whether it was anger or
it was the best damned job of pretending he'd ever seen. A
he knew was, he liked it—and her. And he knew that h
wasn't about to worry about Ryan Malone's future or sto
seeing Sunny Clary, whatever the outcome.

One fan, walking along the greens inside the roped-off are
called out, "Hey, Sunny, saw you on television the night of th
Valentine's fund-raiser. You were talking to Sam and Nikk
Listen to their show every morning. Loved the dress."

"Thanks," she said and kept walking.

"Must be nice to have friends give you a hand," a less kind voice called out. "Did they help you get the job with WTRU? Or was it Mr. Malone?"

"Help me? Of course not. Nobody helped me. Why would you think that?" Sunny frowned, turned toward the speaker and stopped. "It was you back there in the woods."

"Yeah," he said, flicking the strap of the camera hanging around his neck. "I thought since you seem to have an in with the powers that be, we could work out a deal. Your influence for the pictures. I need a job."

"Miss Clary doesn't and never did need anyone's influence to get a job," Ryan snapped, moving to Sunny's side, next to the photographer. What he wanted to do was snap the weasel's head from his neck and stomp on it. But he suspected that he was being deliberately goaded into making just such a move. Instead, he said, "If you've been watching WTRU for the past week, you know that she's the most incredible new talent Atlanta has to offer. And who are you, anyway?"

"Edward Hinton," the man answered with a confident smile. "Here, take my card." He managed to push a card in Ryan's hand. "I'm an excellent photographer. I'm sure I have some great shots of the two of you. Would you like copies?"

Walt, sensing something he didn't understand, took a spot next to Hinton. "Need some help here, Malone?"

Sunny shook her head. "It's nothing, Walt. Let's just keep going."

But Ryan wasn't ready yet. "What paper do you represent, Mr. Hinton?"

"Oh, no special paper, at the moment. I freelance. It's interesting how a person gets lucky every now and then. They wouldn't give me a press pass to follow the players. I had to buy a ticket. Who could have imagined what I'd see in the woods?"

Ryan glanced at his watch, and looked around. Andrews and his caddy were still a distance away, walking toward them. He recognized a shakedown when he saw one. "As a freelancer I suppose you sell your work."

"Of course. And my photographs, too. I also trade information for profit."

"How much?"

"Oh, no!" Sunny said. "You're not buying the story and pictures from this man. I don't approve of blackmail of any kind. If I've done something that is newsworthy, it should be printed. So, go ahead, Mr. Hinton. Sell your piece to the highest bidder. But it won't be me and it won't be Mr. Malone!"

Ryan looked at the woman he'd compromised with his attempt to have lunch. She was magnificent when she was angry but this time she might be wrong. Still, this wasn't the time to argue. He'd take care of the problem later. "She's right, Hinton, and if you don't move along, I'm going to call security."

"You'll be sorry about this, Malone," he said. "I never wanted your money. I just wanted a job." He whirled and disappeared into the trees.

Sunny's full lips were pressed into a thin line as she watched him leave. All Ryan could think about was putting his arms around her and telling her everything would be all right.

"Are you sure you don't want me to buy him off?" he finally asked.

"I'm sure. I came to Atlanta to uncover crime, not commit one. If I've done something shameful, I'll accept the consequences."

"There was nothing shameful about what happened,

Sunny. But I see where it could look bad to the world. And I'm truly sorry. It seems that I'm always saying that to you."

"It wasn't entirely your fault."

"He's right about one thing. People are going to think that I'm buying your way here."

"It isn't that I'm worried about. It's my dad. He's already been crucified in the press for something he didn't do. If Hinton starts spreading his filth to get even, people will find out that Pop was in jail. I don't want him to face that again."

Ryan took her hand. "I won't let that happen if I can help it, Sunny. But you're in the limelight now and nothing is private. I know."

She sighed. "You're right. I'd just hoped that I could have a little more time."

"Sometimes a thing gets out of control," Ryan said quietly, rolling his thumb around inside her palm. He liked being with her, holding her hand. It felt—right. "You know it's happening and there's not a thing you can do to stop it."

The sincere tone in his voice slowed her fury. She looked at him and saw understanding in his eyes. How selfish could a person be? This wasn't just about her, his reputation could be tarnished as well. "Ryan, I'm sorry. I didn't think about what could happen to you. You could be hurt as well. I'll ask Walt to check with the other press people. Somebody might know his address."

"Good idea. I'll put some of my people on it."

Sunny smiled. Up to now, every time something had gone wrong in her life, she'd had to face it alone. Just this once, she had a partner. "Maybe it won't be so bad, Ryan," she said.

"You know something, Sunny? Maybe it doesn't matter. Maybe it's time we both stop worrying about what people think of us. More important people have survived the truth."

"Yeah, tell that to Lord Sin," she quipped.

"Maybe I will," he said. "Maybe I will."

8

EDWARD HINTON DISAPPEARED, but for the rest of the day, Sunny kept her eyes open, looking for the thin man who could ruin her. Walt asked around but nobody had an address.

When Ryan and the Atlanta Braves pitcher, Joe Andrews, won the match it came as no surprise. The check for twenty-five thousand dollars was turned over to Anne Kelley, representative for Doctor's Hospital. And, as predicted, all the golfers retired to the Greenhouse where special prizes provided by the sporting goods manufacturers were distributed. Then came the predicted drinks and wild stories of past glories. Ryan stood at Sunny's shoulder but made no effort to intrude on her duties as a reporter. When Sunny had gotten the required statement from Joe Andrews and a thank-you from Anne Kelley, she headed toward the exit.

She needed calm and space—anywhere away from Ryan Malone. She thought she was going to make it when Ryan caught up with them.

"Don't worry about what happened," he said. "This will work out."

"Yeah, that's what I always thought. I was wrong. It's not your fault, Malone, but the last problem I had got me fired."

"Ted Fields isn't going to fire you."

"I didn't think my last boss would fire me either, but he did. I gotta get back to the station. Thanks for the lunch."

"Tomorrow night, Sunny. The address is 3148 Peachtree

Road, penthouse suite. I'll tell the security guard to expect you and your father about six o'clock."

"Are you sure? Ryan, I think we ought to call that off."

"No way. I've bought enough food to feed half the television station. Besides, if you don't come, Lottie will have my head." He took her hand and held it for just a moment, looking deep into her eyes. "I didn't plan on us, Sunny. Didn't expect it. But I'm not letting Edward Hinton spoil whatever we have. You and I are more important than that."

Then, as if his previous actions hadn't been compromising enough, he reached down and kissed her, a quick goodbye kiss that promised they weren't done yet.

"Trust me," he said with a smile. "You haven't seen all my talents yet."

All his talents. On the way back to the station she chewed on that statement. She told herself she wasn't sure she wanted to. And she knew she was lying. Thank goodness her father would be there tomorrow night. She would need a head clearer than her own. If Edward Hinton sold the picture of Ryan fondling her breasts in the woods, it could ruin everything for her. At the same time, she refused to allow Ryan to "fix" the problem by buying the photograph. If Ted fired her, at least she'd have faced the problem straight on.

A far greater threat to her peace of mind was Ryan Malone. Could she afford to let their relationship develop any further? Did she even want that? She let out a sigh. Who was she kidding? She wanted him as much as she wanted her career. Dammit, why couldn't she have both?

"YOU'RE DOING A FINE JOB, Sunny," Ted Fields said as she turned in her story on the golf tournament. "You got pictures of the stars, interviews with the winners and made the folks in Atlanta say, 'Ahh!' over the money raised for all those children whose families can't afford to pay hospital fees. I never would have thought that good news would excite our viewers."

"Sure, and which part of the story do you think they're excited about, the children, Joe Andrews, or Ryan Malone and the 'Good-News Girl'?"

"Sunny and Ryan, of course. It's human nature, my girl. Viewers always go for the stars. Why do you think they invite them to play in the tournaments?"

Sunny sighed in frustration. "Ted, I need to talk to you. Something happened today that...could jeopardize my position here. It involves Ryan Malone."

"If you're worried about your relationship with Ryan Malone, don't."

"I am worried. It isn't just the relationship." She hesitated, trying to find the right words, then decided there weren't any. "Today there was an incident—with a honeybee—in the woods. Malone had to get it out of—"

"Get it?" Ted prompted.

Sunny took a deep breath. "Out of my shirt."

"I see," Ted said, seriously, "And how is that going to affect your career at WTRU?"

"Someone photographed us, a freelance journalist who seems to think it will reflect badly on my reputation as a journalist. Stop and think. So far, I've been with Ryan Malone in every on-the-air story I've done: the Valentine Ball, the nursing home party, the golf tournament. It looks as if the wealthiest bachelor in Atlanta is my protector, as if he's providing the news for me to cover. That's bad enough. But now it appears that he's—fondling me in public."

"And the fans will probably love it."

"But the people whose respect I have to earn to do my job won't," she argued.

Ted pushed his glasses up his nose and pursed his lips. "What does Malone say?"

"Actually, he asked the man what he wanted, if the pictures were for sale. They are for sale to the highest bidder."

That made Ted angry. "Professional blackmail! What's the weasel's name?"

"That's what I called him. His name is Edward Hinton."

Ted groaned. "To call that man a weasel is to insult the weasel. He's been fired from at least one newspaper and one television station for, let's call it, manufacturing news. If you hear from him again, tell him to give me a call."

"You're not going to buy the picture, Ted. I won't allow that. I'll resign and find a job as a..." she thought about Lord Sin and finished "...janitor, if I have to."

"It isn't illegal to buy photographs," Ted admitted. "Don't worry. There's not much that we haven't had to deal with. I admit this might look bad but I can't see what harm it can do for the viewers to know you're romantically involved with Malone—if you are. If we're talking careers, it can't hurt his and I'm thinking that it won't hurt yours. Let's don't get worried yet. Are you getting settled in?" he asked, changing the subject.

"I suppose. So far I've not had a lot of time to spend in my apartment, but my dad's coming in tomorrow for a few days."

"I'd like to meet him," Ted said. "Bring him by the station."

"I will," Sunny agreed, her mind still reeling from her day. She'd started with Ryan Malone, then run head-on into Edward Hinton. She'd already decided that Hinton was an opportunist. About Ryan, she was totally confused.

SUNNY SPENT THE AFTERNOON checking out running trails, settling on one that hugged the bank of the Chattahoochee River. Though it was late February, the trail had enough joggers to make her feel safe without being so crowded that she lost the pleasure of the solitude. Plaques along the river marked battle sites from the Civil War. Magnolia trees dotted the hilly terrain, along with huge water oaks and stately loblolly pines. The dirt here wasn't sandy like her favorite running spots in south Georgia. Instead, the soil was dark and rich, broken here and there by gashes of red Georgia clay and clusters of wild azaleas already budding and ready to bloom in a few months.

The path was well maintained, allowing her to set a steady pace, the rhythm a kind of hypnotic meditation. She needed that. In a week's time she'd traversed the roller coaster of emotion that came from a new town, a new job, her sensual reaction to a male stripper and the unexpected feeling of belonging that had come over her since Ryan Malone intruded in her life. Now she was committed to having dinner with him tomorrow night. At least, with Lottie and her father along, they wouldn't be alone. She didn't trust herself to be alone with the tycoon. But, she justified, she wanted her father to meet Ryan, didn't she?

Finally, the approaching dusk forced her to turn around. She covered the last half-mile in a walk, making it back to her car just as the final rays of sun disappeared. She was tired, but she felt better. Ted was right. Edward Hinton couldn't hurt her. In fact, she might just make him her next investigation—after Lord Sin.

Lord Sin. That name took her thoughts in another direction. Tonight, on her way home, she'd stop for take-out Chinese and watch the rest of his tape. By now, Sin ought to know enough about her to decide whether or not to grant her an interview. She'd given Ryan Malone ample opportunity to get her into his bed and he'd failed. Why didn't that make her feel good? From now on, she was on her own. She'd find the mystery man without any help.

What she didn't expect was to find Ryan Malone sitting on her top step.

"What are you doing here?" she asked.

"I wanted to see you. I hope you like Chinese," he said slowly, letting his gaze capture hers, then slide down her body until he caught sight of the paper bag and the carton of noodles she was carrying.

She couldn't help it. A warm rush of pleasure washed over her traitorous body. She liked him. She was glad he had come. In spite of her arguments to the contrary, she wanted to see him—no, needed to see him. At the same time, finding him here waiting was disturbing. She didn't know what to say. Catching sight of his carry-out containers, she stood there, smiling like a dope. "Chinese? Yeah, I do."

"Good. Another thing we have in common. May I come in?"

She hesitated, then nodded. "I guess. But it would have been better if you'd called first."

"I was afraid you'd say no."

"I probably would have," she said as he stood when she slid past him, feeling the instant response of her nipples grazing his chest as she opened the door and turned on the lamp inside.

"That's what I thought. What else do you like to eat?"

"Pork and beans."

"Another common interest. We like the same food. We're both ambitious. Neither of us knew our fathers or know how to fish. That's a pretty good start. At least it works for me. And, Sunny—"

"You like me. Admit it, Malone. You like me."

He nodded. "I do."

"And," she went on, enjoying the uncertainty she was seeing in his face, "with or without Hinton's pictures, we're the hottest couple in Atlanta right now."

"We definitely are. I used to hear kids say that if they were going to be accused of doing something anyway, they might as well get the benefit of the act. How do you feel about living up to your potential?"

"Don't joke about it, Malone. Just tell me what you're doing here. Why did you come?"

He looked around the spotless apartment, taking in the personal touches she'd given the place. Bright colored cushions, candles, books and— "Puzzles? You put picture puzzles together?"

"I do. At least my father and I used to do that."

"I did, too, once, when I lived..." He swallowed the rest of his sentence. He had lived with a family once where the grandmother always had a puzzle on her coffee table. She'd been lonely, too old to fit into the young family, and he'd felt a kinship there, for a time. Then he'd been moved to another home and there were never any picture puzzles again. He didn't know why he'd never bought any. But Sunny had.

She took the cardboard containers into the tiny kitchen. He could hear her opening cabinets and rattling dishes. "When you lived where, Malone? Were you born in Atlanta?"

"Yes, I'm one of those rare born and bred Atlantans. What about you?"

"Albany, Georgia. That's 'All-Benny' to the people who live there. Two years at Valdosta State and a degree from the University of Georgia in Communications and Journalism." The conversation was normal but there was nothing natural about the currents swirling around the small apartment. She had to do something.

Sunny took a soft drink from the refrigerator, walked back into the room, handed the can to Ryan and kept going. "Sorry, don't have anything stronger. If you'd like to eat your food, go ahead. I'm going to shower now and eat later."

As quickly as she could, she scurried into her bedroom and closed the door.

Ryan took a sip from the icy can, trying to moisten his dry throat. The apartment was certainly big enough for one person, but it suddenly seemed too small for two. He slid out of his jacket and draped it over Sunny's on the back of the chair and wandered over to her stereo. Mozart, the sound track from *Titanic*, Celine Dion, Neil Diamond, Elton John and— he grinned—George Jones? The woman had interesting musical taste, not too different from his own. He slid the Celine Dion tape into the player and touched the on button.

The sound of water splashing pulled his thoughts back to Sunny, of her bare breasts, of the feel of her skin beneath the lace of her bra. If she were any other woman, by now they'd be showering together. He tightened his grip on the can. No woman had ever kept him at bay this long or kept him as interested. It had to be her resistance that attracted him to her. He couldn't be falling for her. He just wanted to make love to her. Once he'd done that, the need would go away, or as Lottie had said, his itch would be scratched. The sooner that happened, the better—for both of them. Then his life would go back to normal.

He continued his stroll around her living room. Bookshelves filled with an even wider selection than his own. She read everything from horror to nonfiction. Politics seemed to be a favorite topic. Casually, he pulled down a book praising Richard Nixon's contributions to history, thumbed through it and gave a laugh. The woman not only read her books, she argued with them. In red pen, all around the margins she'd scribbled her disagreement with his policies. Never one to pass up a debate, he jotted a few rebuttal remarks, then swapped Nixon for a gossipy tell-all about Princess Diana. Here the arguments were supportive of the Princess, as Ryan would have expected.

It was the scrapbook of newspaper clippings that took him to the easy chair by the table lamp. It was the scrapbook that told him what had made Sunny Clary run. Headlines read: Local Accountant Suspected Of Wrongdoing. And Byron Clary Takes Kickbacks. He'd heard Sunny tell Lottie about her father but the harsh accounting of his trouble explained a lot. Sunny's father had been the controller for a large government contractor whose buildings dotted the state. Guilty of buying inferior products and padding the expense sheets, the company and its partners in the wrongdoing had made millions. And Byron Clary signed off on the purchase orders. Kickbacks had been paid and cancelled checks made out to Clary seemed to prove his guilt.

Sunny's father had gone to jail. The company had failed. And months later, the owner had drowned in a boating accident. The politicians who'd awarded the contracts went unscathed.

A sound caught Ryan's attention and he looked up. Sunny, wearing a white robe, was standing in her bedroom door, leaning forward to towel dry her hair. There was something Elizabethan about red hair against all that white.

"Are you still here?" she asked, without turning her gaze to him.

"Yes. I've been looking at your books. You have an interesting collection."

"I like to read. It makes me think. What makes you think?"

He ran his fingers through his hair and tried to answer her. He really did. But all he could think about at the moment was that she was nude under that robe. That the breasts he'd seen yesterday were free.

"What's wrong? Did my question leave you speechless?"

At that moment his stomach growled. Not a gentle little reminder growl, but a roar designed to get attention. "I'm having a hard time thinking about anything except my stomach," he said.

"Do you think about your stomach a lot?" she asked.

"Well, not as much as I think about my other body parts. Actually, the stomach is probably one of the most demanding but least attractive, conversationally and sensually, that is."

She raised up and wrapped her towel around her hair. "Are you all right, Malone?"

One corner of his mouth curled up. "Not really."

From the look in his eyes, Sunny realized she'd made an error. She should have pulled on a sweatshirt, maybe a suit of armor. She should have forced him to go, feigning a necessity to work or her need for sleep after a long day. Now it was too late.

Malone folded the book he was reading and laid it back on the table, then stood up. His gaze was planted squarely on her breasts and she realized that when she'd leaned over to rub her hair, the folds of her robe must have gaped open. "Let me throw some clothes on and I'll nuke the noodles. Then you really have to go."

"What's the matter, Sunny, are you scared?"

She gave a laugh, trying to neutralize the charge of the atmosphere between them. "Scared? Yes, I think I am."

He took a step closer. "Don't laugh, country girl, I'm scared, too. We've both been heading for this moment from the beginning. Stop fighting what we feel." He'd been tense when he first looked up at her, but now that tension seemed to melt, slowing his speech, lowering his voice. "You're beautiful. You're smart. You've had to scrap to get where you are. We match." He took another step forward, she another step back until they were both at her bedroom door.

"I want to see your knit sheets, darling."

"I don't have them anymore," she said, walking around to

the other side of the bed and pulling down the comforter. "See?"

"Cotton? Plain cotton?" Following her around the bed, he shook his head in mock disbelief. "So, you lied to me. Did you lie about the other stuff as well?"

"Other stuff?"

He took her face in his hands, holding it gently, studying it as though he'd never seen a face before. "The perfume," he said, "and the smile?"

She twisted away. "Go home, Malone. Please?"

"Please? Please, kiss you? I couldn't stop myself if I wanted to. Let me, Sunny. Just a kiss. One kiss?"

"Will you go?"

He nodded.

She didn't stop him as he covered her mouth with his own in a gentle, persistent tug. When her lips opened, he slipped his tongue inside, caressing her inner warmth in rhythm to the pulsing of the erection that came even before he touched her. For a long minute they stayed like that, then, without releasing her lips, his fingers moved down the collar of the robe to the tightly drawn sash at her waist. He loosened it and let the robe fall open as he pulled away.

"No!" she whispered, grabbing at the edges of her robe. "You said you'd go."

Then his shirt was unbuttoned and her hand was inside, hot against his skin. Her breasts were pert, her nipples peaked against his palm. He let go for a moment, shifting his shoulders so that his shirt was gone completely and he was rewarded by the tentative touch of her fingertips. He groaned.

She stopped, laid her forehead against his chin and drew in a deep breath. What was happening here? After all her plans to avoid involvement, she was standing here, practically nude, touching him—inviting him... "Don't do this, Malone."

"Only what you want me to," he said as he slipped the robe from her shoulders and let it fall to the floor.

He reached out and touched her breast, skimming it lightly, starting a thousand fires just beneath the skin, fires that ran down every pulsing vein in her body and settled between her legs. Ryan didn't try to hide his erection. Instead, he unzipped his trousers and let them fall. Then pulled her hard against him. "I have to make love to you, Sunny. We both have to know if this is just a fantasy Sin started, or if it's real."

Her knees were trembling. Her breath was wild and her heart pounded like tom-toms in an exotic island movie. Then, as if they were being orchestrated by some unseen director on that movie set, her fingers tugged down the top of his briefs and his erection sprang free. His eyes churned with desire, yet he didn't speak. She looked at him and caught her breath.

He picked her up and laid her on the bed, coming down beside her. "Why'd you change them?"

"What?"

"The sheets?"

"So you wouldn't be here in bed with me every night. Once I told you about my bed, I couldn't get you out of it."

"And you thought this would erase me?"

"I hoped."

"Didn't work, did it?"

He leaned over her, taking one nipple into his mouth. Sunny moaned and a tiny shudder ran through her. Emotion crashed over her and she couldn't still her hands from running through his hair. Then they were holding him to her, asking for more. He'd been right. From the first time she looked at him it had been destined. This had to happen. She let go of her last reserves, knowing, with what little reason she had left, that she was about to become one of Ryan Malone's women. He would make love to her, move on and, if what she'd been told was true, they'd simply become friends. Perhaps that was her only way out.

So be it.

Sunny closed her eyes, submerging herself into nothing but pure sensation. His mouth left her breasts and claimed her lips once more and the heat, already spiraling out of control, intensified. When he finally pulled back, his eyes were stormy black. "Sunny?"

"You said your bed or mine," she whispered. "This is mine."

Ryan took a deep breath and cursed under his breath. No condom. He hadn't expected this. He hadn't even come prepared and that was totally unlike him. Now her body was melting beneath him. This time she was going with him, and she was in charge of the trip. He couldn't stop. There was no way in hell he could stop. The tumult raging inside him was new. He wanted to please Sunny but it was more than just sex. His hands were actually trembling.

"You said this wouldn't happen until I wanted it. Well, I want it."

He looked down at her breasts, full and tanned. The site of the beesting was still obvious. He kissed it. "Are you sure?" he murmured, touching his lips to hers. "You're very beautiful. Nipples all pink and swollen, begging to be kissed." His lips encased one nipple and gently pulled on it. Letting it go and taking it back again, while his hands capped her shoulders, circling them in heated caresses. As he moved his mouth across her in a slow, rapt examination of her neck and breasts, he whispered to her constantly.

"Your skin looks as if it's been touched by the sun—golden and warm."

She couldn't understand the gentleness of his lips, his tongue, his body. To support his weight he'd moved one leg over her legs, pressing the evidence of his desire against her. He kissed her again and moved a bit more, until she could feel it pulsating against that part of her now drenched in moisture.

She moaned, trembling now with excitement as his fingertips ranged lower. His lips captured her mouth as he found the source of the moisture. His fingers caressed her, sliding across, around and finally inside her. She groaned and pushed the aching part of her against him.

"Patience, my love," he whispered between kisses. "I want to make love to you. I want you to feel my mouth on yours, to draw the sweet taste of you into mine, to caress your nipples." His kisses moved down her body with his lips, tasting, licking, memorizing every part of her. Until, to her shock, his lips found her ache. She jerked, trying to move away. And then she felt the trembling intensify and her moan turned into a tight groan as an incredible, primitive wave of unrelenting heat racked her body. When the surge of her convulsions eventually died away, Ryan lay across her, his face against her stomach.

Dazed from the aftermath of the fiery explosion, Sunny lay limp and stunned. Only the sound of slow and labored breathing and the sweet voice of Celine Dion filled the apartment. Finally, knowledge and embarrassment forced her to speak. "Forget what I said."

"About what?" he asked.

"You don't need any lessons from Lord Sin."

"I don't?"

Another long silence. Sunny didn't feel Ryan's erection against her, but he hadn't satisfied it and she knew she hadn't given him what he'd given her. "Malone—"

"Couldn't you call me Ryan?"

She could, but not now. Ryan was tender. Ryan was sharing. What had just happened was...what? She didn't know yet. "Malone," she repeated, "what about you?"

"What about me?" he asked in a husky voice.

"I mean...you didn't. You're still...aren't you?"

"Oh, yes. I didn't and I still am." He pulled back and rested his upper body on one elbow as he looked down at her. "There's just one little problem. I didn't expect this and I didn't come prepared to make love to you. So unless you have something in that nightstand drawer, I'm going to forget about loving you all night, put on my clothes and get the hell out of here." He groaned and added, "I won't make that mistake again."

"Again?" she whispered, as much to herself as to him.

"The next time, it'll be in my bed and I won't stop loving you until we're both too sated to move—if that's what you want." He leaned over, kissed both her breasts, her mouth and then closed her eyes with his mouth. It was harder than he could have imagined. But Ryan knew he had to give Sunny time. He already knew what he wanted.

If that's what I want? Sunny didn't open her eyes. She only listened as he rose from her bed and pulled on his clothes. Then came the sound of her door closing and the strains of a Celine Dion song echoing in the silence.

She knew what she wanted but she had to be sure.

RYAN GLANCED AT HIS WATCH. It wasn't too late. He stilled his breathing, reached down and picked up his car phone, then dialed a number.

A ring, then, "Hello?"

"About that doll, Lottie. How do I blow her up?"

"You've been with Sunny?" she asked.

"Yes."

"And?" Lottie prompted.

"If you think I'm going to share the details of our evening, forget it. Just let me say, she's still technically untouched."

"Sounds like you are, too."

"My own choice," he admitted. "And that's the problem. Lottie, this time, I'm swimming in deep waters."

She gave a measured, "Mmm."

"You're not much help."

"Nope. This time you're on your own."

"She's special, Lottie. I didn't expect this. I've only known her a few days and she's got me thinking about things I don't want to think about."

"A sinner like you, thinking about a ring and a preacher?"

"I don't know," he said, quietly adding, "Maybe."

Lottie let out a real chortle. "I knew it. Speaking of preachers, I can't wait to meet her father. If he's half the man I expect him to be, I'm really going to enjoy dinner tomorrow night."

"Lottie! Behave yourself. The man's a minister."

"Yeah, but he was a sinner first."

9

THE CHINESE FOOD was still on the counter when Sunny pulled on her robe and stumbled to the kitchen the next morning. The paper bag she'd dropped on the counter lay on its side, a cellophane bag containing a fortune cookie spilling out. As if she were sleepwalking, Sunny heated hot water in the microwave, spooned in instant coffee and powdered cream and stood at the sink drinking it.

Through the window, the sun, bright and intrusive, was high in the sky. She'd never expected to sleep. But she had, and she'd slept better than she had in months. So long as she continued simply to feel, without thinking about what happened last night, she'd be fine. And for now, the feeling was delicious. The corners of her lips were curved into a smile. She felt...the word finally came to her—alive. She really could run the Peachtree Road Race this morning. Draining her cup, she set it on the counter, then picked up the fortune cookie and ripped open the packet.

Fate takes you down a dangerous path.

There was something chillingly familiar about those words. Lord Sin had used them. She tugged the sash of her robe tighter. But the warm thrum of her body didn't give way to the expected tight anxiety that should have made her face what she'd done. Nothing could erase the memory of having Ryan Malone touch her with his lips. She didn't think it was the talent Lottie had referred to, but if they'd been giving out medals, she'd have given him a gold. This morning, her body was still singing. It was her mind that stumbled on the beat. But no matter what it said, she knew it had been special. Malone was special. Whatever other talents he had, he was a caring man, the kind any woman would choose.

And for now, for a while, he'd chosen her. Maybe she was being foolish, but for today she refused to feel either guilt or remorse. Her path was of her own making and she intended to walk it.

Later she found her scrapbook on the table beside the chair. Ryan had been reading about her father when she'd walked back into the living room wearing only her robe. With a groan, she returned the book to the shelf. Now he knew everything about her father, and how he'd been branded a criminal. The only thing he didn't know was what happened to get her fired. And she didn't know a thing about him except he had been born in Atlanta and didn't know who his father was.

And that he knew how to make love to a woman.

But you do know him, she argued with herself. You may not know the specifics, but you are learning about Ryan's good qualities. Before, she'd had doubts about the men she'd slept with. She'd thought at the time that the doubts were about herself. She'd been wrong. Knowing Ryan Malone had taught her what she liked about a man. What he stood for was what counted. And, she smiled, it didn't hurt to have talent.

Sunny moved over to her nightstand and pulled open the drawer. Inside were three condom packets. If she trusted him, why hadn't she told him?

RYAN WOKE WITH A SMILE on his face. He was willing to admit that being with Sunny had been a truly earth-moving experience. But he'd thought he'd had awesome experiences before. And sooner or later, the awe had worn off and both partners had moved on. He told himself that would happen with Sunny. He told himself, but he knew he was lying. Sunny in his bed had been his goal but now that he'd reached that—more or less—he knew he wanted more.

The stories about Sunny's father weighed on his mind. He went to his home office and picked up the phone. It didn't take long to satisfy himself that Sunny's father had been framed. It was his call to the newspaper where she'd been employed that provided the most interesting information. The editor thought Ryan was considering hiring Sunny and, keeping the legalities of their parting of the ways in mind, suggested that Sunny was very good at investigative reporting if that's what Ryan wanted.

"But?" Ryan prodded.

"But, sometimes, she needs a bit of control. As a businessman, I'm sure you know that at times, it is necessary for a few to be sacrificed for the good of all, hypothetically speaking, of course."

"No, I don't," Ryan said in a deadly low voice. "The sacrificing of just one person is never more important than the good of all."

Sunny would never have sacrificed her principles. If she had, it must have had something to do with her father.

Ryan sat at his breakfast table, drinking the last of his coffee and feeling it burn his stomach like lye. Sacrifice. His mother had been sacrificed for the good of the family of the man she'd fallen in love with. He was meant for great things, local politics, then Washington, and possibly the White House. So they'd tried to pay her off with legalese and threats. But she'd stood up to them in the beginning. The scandal and her pregnancy had cost her her career. Money had covered up his father's sins. Ryan had been too young then to understand why his mother cried, then drank, and finally gave herself up to the haze of drugs that took away the pain. When the department of children's services came for him, she was too far gone to know. And as a frightened five-year-old he was relegated to foster care for the next eleven years.

Ryan was finally going to redeem his mother's life. The children's hospital wing would offer hope and help to women like her. It would be called The Helen Malone Center for Women and Children, named for his mother.

He'd take Sunny to the dedication. She'd understand what he was doing. Then he gave a dry laugh. The Good-News Girl would likely be there on her own to cover the ceremonies for WTRU, not by his side as his lady.

After what happened yesterday in the woods, she probably wouldn't go with him anywhere. The incident with the bee would have been amusing under other conditions but in the wrong hands, with the wrong words, the interpretation could be harmful. He'd have to find a way to suppress the photographs. A quick call to an associate in the investigative services field set the first part of his plan in motion. Information about Edward Hinton and where to find him. The next call was to Lottie to set the second part of his plan in motion.

Ryan hadn't been able to protect his mother, but as Lord Sin he'd learned how to protect himself. Now he had to do the same for Sunny. Rising, he walked over to the window and looked out on the sprawling city of Atlanta. It didn't seem to know which way it wanted to go and had grown willy-nilly, sprinkling buildings and restaurants among old homes that still belonged to the families who'd built them in the late eighteen hundreds.

Sunny would have loved the Atlanta of his youth, before skyscrapers replaced so many of those mansions. The bright morning spears of light cast a warmth across the rooftops. A warmth that made him think of Sunny. He'd held her, made love to her and, to his own surprise, he'd stopped short of taking her completely. As a child, on the rare occasions when he'd been given sweets, he'd deprived himself of the pleasure by rationing the candy so that it would last. Sunny was one of the ultimate sweets and he was willing to wait.

First he had to meet her father. Lottie would be there to cushion any awkwardness—he hoped. God only knew what she'd do. Instead of following his wishes that she help him feed Sunny a false story about Lord Sin, she'd given her a videotape. And now Sunny had seen it. He wanted to strangle Lottie. For the first time in their relationship, he didn't trust Lottie. She'd probably climb up on the table and give the Reverend Clary a demonstration of bump and grind.

He read the newspaper and spent an hour in his gym. It didn't help. His body was still remembering the erotic vision in his arms the night before and it was simply waiting. Finally, he pulled out his cookbooks and began the preparation of their meal. He opened the spice drawer and grinned. Sunny must think of him as a complete dufus, not even able to use a screwdriver. He could have, had he not been so involved in listening to what Lottie was telling Sunny. Sunny the handyman, who'd made herself daddy's girl, but never felt close to him, who couldn't cook, kissed like an angel and wouldn't let go of Lord Sin.

He could picture her now, in her white robe, drying her magnificently wild mane of red hair. He'd bet it wasn't just her height that brought an end to her career as a gymnast, those breasts had to have interfered with her performance. Training to be an athlete and then being forced to give it up must not have been easy. He liked making money in real estate but Lord Sin's last performance had been surprisingly satisfying.

Becoming a reporter had to have been Sunny's way of making it up to her father for the terrible thing that had hapened to him. She'd had a goal and she'd thrown herself into reaching it. Now Edward Hinton had threatened to sell the photographs to one of the national exposé magazines. She was right to worry about her credibility. He also had his own to worry about.

For now, he just had to keep his name out of the news until after the dedication of the hospital wing next week. Then e'd allow Sunny to learn the story he'd created to explain ord Sin's disappearance. The photo he'd set up last year would be the proof of Sin's presence on the Riviera. She'd report it as a small human interest story that, once aired, would soon be forgotten. Then he could move on with his life.

Except now there was Sunny. He could move on with his fe, but he couldn't leave her behind. And if he didn't find Hinton, Sunny's career might be at risk.

For now, he had to prepare a meal. Cooking lessons had been another area he'd spent money in during what he called his formative years. Golf, to be able to keep up with the young executives on the go, and the preparation of food because as a child he'd been hungry more often than not.

A simple salad with a dressing made from Georgia's famous Vidalia onions would start the meal. Without knowing the Reverend Clary's tastes, he'd elected to go with the average man's preference for pork, preparing medallions of tenderloin marinated in his own special blend of herbs, broiled new potatoes, green beans and another of his specialties, skillet-baked cornbread. Filling his thoughts with the preparation of food would keep him from thinking about Sunny. At least that's what he told himself.

The beans were snapped. The pork and the potatoes were in the pan, ready to be broiled. And the cornbread ingredients were mixed, except for the liquids. For dessert, fresh fruit and ice cream with a raspberry sauce. At five-thirty the cooking would begin. He glanced around, pleased with his kitchen and the adjacent dining area.

The table was set. Candles were ready to be lit. He flipped on the wraparound stereo system that fed music throughout the house and headed for the shower. Fifteen minutes later he sat on his bed, tugged on his socks and stood, automatically smoothing out the wrinkles in his comforter. Knit sheets. She'd removed them from her bed so she wouldn't picture him in it. Replacing them with cotton sheets hadn't kept that from happening. He studied his king-size bed and felt its emptiness without Sunny.

The next CD clicked into place. The singer was Celine Dion. Where had that CD come from?

When the doorbell rang, Ryan headed toward it, barefoot and still buttoning his shirt. Behind the door was Lottie beaming brightly. "Am I the first?"

"It's only five-thirty. You know you're the first."

Lottie took a long look at Ryan's shirt and trousers. "Don't you think you ought to wear a tie—and shoes?" She followed him inside.

"Why? This isn't a formal dinner. My apron is about as dressed up as I get," he said, lifting a green apron from a hook inside the pantry door and tying it around his waist.

"Green?" Lottie said with a grin.

"Green," he said.

"And no slits. Shoot, she's going to be disappointed."

"Lottie, behave yourself. We don't know Mr. Clary. He might not be a man who appreciates levity."

"Then I'll become Mother Teresa. Where's my habit?"

"Lottie! If the subject of Lord Sin comes up, it's time for us to start setting up our story. If it doesn't, don't mention him."

"Yes, sir. Something smells good. What are we having?"

"Pork and beans and potatoes," he said and waited for the question in her eyes.

"Pork and beans? Pooh. I was hoping for oysters. Want me to give you a hand?"

"I do not. You can light the candles, if you want. And change that CD."

"Celine Dion? I like her. What's wrong with her music? She sings like an angel."

"Yeah, and she's looking for love."

"Ain't we all."

"SO, TELL ME ABOUT your fella," Byron Clary said as Sunny drove down the drive past the big columned house and accelerated out into Peachtree Street.

"He's not my fella. He's just a man I keep running into."

"Yeah, I can see that from your speed."

Sunny glanced down at her speed and let her foot off the gas. "Sorry, Pop. I'm just a little out of kilter here. So much has happened so fast."

"You mean with Mr. Malone, or with the job?"

"At the moment they seem to be the same thing. You've heard of the Kevin Bacon theory on six degrees of separation?"

Her father looked confused. "No, can't say that I have."

"It's based on the idea that you can bring up any actor and by naming six movies, he can be connected to the actor Kevin Bacon."

She could tell that her explanation was creating more questions than answers. "Never mind, let's just say that every story I've covered has in some way involved Ryan Malone."

"Is he some important person?"

"Yes, he is."

Mr. Clary looked down at his casual shoes and jacket. "Are you sure I'm dressed up enough for a VIP?"

Sunny glanced at her own jeans and grinned. "Look at me, Pop. Do I look dressed up?"

"No, but when I see those folks at the Country Music Awards going up to collect their honors in jeans and a tuxedo jacket, I know that I'm completely out of style."

"You look great," Sunny said, reaching out and squeezing his hand. They shared a new closeness since he'd found his church. Gone was the tired, work-driven man who had little time for a little girl. "I'm so glad you're here, and you're going to love Lottie."

Mr. Clary cut a sharp glance at his daughter. "Lottie? Who is Lottie?"

"She's a friend of..." she started to say Lord Sin, then changed it to "...a very good friend of Ryan Malone." She knew her father was an open-minded man but explaining Lord Sin and the attraction women had for him was more than she could manage right now. "Help me watch for the number, Pop. It should be along here somewhere."

"But these are office buildings," he said.

"Exactly. We're looking for the Malone Building. It will be on your side."

"The Malone Building?" he questioned. "As in our host Malone?"

"That's him. He has a penthouse on the top floor."

Byron Clary laughed. "A penthouse in the sky. My, my. Your mother would have been so pleased."

"I couldn't have done it without you, Pop."

"But you did, Sunny. And you shouldn't have had to."

Then she spotted the building, slowed her speed and turned into the parking area beneath where she was met by a security guard. "Miss Clary," he said. "Mr. Malone is expecting you. If you'll just pull into that reserved spot, ma'am. Take the elevator to the lobby and someone will unlock the elevator to the penthouse."

"Thank you," she said, trying to fight off the blush of embarrassment. The guard acted as if she did this frequently.

"And ma'am," he added, "I saw you dancing with Mr. Malone at that nursing home. You two sure looked good."

Sunny groaned and gave the car too much gas, eliciting a squeal from her tires and a smothered grin from her father. "It was a story, Pop. I went to cover a birthday party Mr. Malone was hosting for a...lady who turned one hundred."

"Uh-huh. Since when do reporters dance with the host? Isn't that considered a no-no?"

"It is. I shouldn't have done it. And that's what I need your advice on. First it was a fund-raiser for a new community theater arranged by Mr. Malone. Then the birthday party. Next I was sent to cover the mayor's Inner City Awards dinner, and guess who was receiving a humanitarian award? Ryan Malone. Then yesterday, I had a real assignment, a charity golf tournament in which Mr. Malone was playing. The viewers think he's my sponsor."

"Is he?"

Sunny parked the car and turned off the engine. "No. Though *he* seems to think he is. Every time I'm with him, I end up on camera. Let's go."

Her father followed, a curious look on his face. "Does this mean that we'll be videotaped at dinner?"

"No!" Her voice was firm, but given the situation, she wasn't sure. In fact, it wouldn't hurt for her to go home and check her bedroom for hidden cameras.

"You going to tell me why you accepted this dinner invitation?" her father asked as they stepped into the elevator and the doors closed.

"It started out because I'm working on a story that I thought Mr. Malone and Lottie could help me with."

"And now?"

"Now? Uh, Pop, I don't know."

"What you really want is to know what I think about him, isn't it?" her father asked. "Why, you never asked what I thought before. What's happened to all that fierce independence?"

That stopped her. Was he right? In her attempt to survive her mother's death, had she closed him out? "I don't know. I don't seem to be so sure about things now."

The doors opened onto a black marble lobby, bathed in a golden glow of light.

"Over here, Ms. Clary," the guard said. "I've unlocked the elevator to the penthouse. Mr. Malone is expecting you."

As they moved into the new elevator, Byron Clary cleared his throat. "I'm surprised he didn't just send a chariot and six bearers to pick you up and carry you. I've never felt quite so much out of place."

"I know exactly what you mean."

The elevator moved smoothly up and its doors whispered open directly into a marble foyer outside an ornate brass door. The door was standing open, revealing a large living room decorated in shades of cream and gray with a touch of navy. Brass accessories and lamps gave a feel of warmth to the room. That, and the smell of something wonderful.

"Hello?" Sunny called out, uncertain how to react when an elevator delivered you to an open foyer and an empty room.

"Ryan," Lottie's excited voice called out, "they're here."

Moments later, Sunny was enfolded in Lottie's arms. "Good! You came. I was afraid you'd get cold feet."

"Cold feet?" Sunny questioned.

Lottie drew back and studied Sunny. "Never mind, that's never going to happen, is it?" The silver-haired woman gave Sunny a wink and turned to her father. "I'm Lottie," she said, "and you must be Byron. Bedroom eyes and a romantic name. Must cause you a lot of trouble as a minister." She slid er arm through his and looked up at him with a smile that seemed to stop Reverend Clary where he stood.

"Well, doesn't it?" she asked. "Never mind. Your being a minister won't bother me so long as you're romantic when you're with me. Deal?"

Sunny stared in amazement as her father tilted his head, smiled and put his rough hand over Lottie's. "Deal," he said.

"Fine," Lottie said, "I'll introduce you to Ryan in a minute, but first, let me show you around while those two say hello."

In seconds, they'd disappeared from sight, Lottie chattering and Byron Clary with an expression that clearly said he'd been transported.

"Sorry, Sunny," Ryan's voice said from the doorway across the room. "There, I'm doing it again, apologizing. I told Lottie to behave. I knew she wouldn't listen, but I'll admit, I never expected...this."

"Neither did I," Sunny agreed and started toward him. Her expression must be a reflection of her father's. All she had to do was look at Ryan and she felt like warm caramel inside. She hadn't known what to expect either, but Ryan shoeless and wearing an apron wasn't what she might have envisioned. For one brief moment, she could even see him with a baby in his arms. Brief, for as she got closer, she envisioned him in a different way—heading with her to his bedroom.

"I'm glad you came," he said, taking her hand to draw her into the hallway. He leaned against the royal-blue patterned paper and pulled her close. "I missed you. You are so beautiful."

She gazed up at him, drinking in the dangerous look of his dark hair and eyes. "So are you," she said and knew she should back away, but couldn't. Instead, she lifted her mouth to his.

His kiss started out soft, almost shy, and she melted into

him as he claimed her mouth completely. And the kiss was a
million times more than she'd imagined. Finally, he pulled
back. "If you hadn't come, I'd have been knocking on your
door, papa or not."

"Pop! Oh my goodness." She blushed. Realization of
where they were and how easily she'd given herself to his
touch took away her poise. "What must he think?"

"If I know Lottie," he answered, "and if what I saw was
any indication of her interest, I suspect he's thinking about
the same thing I am. I mean ministers do like women, don't
they?"

"Of course. I mean he's a minister, but he's a man—at least
I think he likes women. He never dated when I was growing
up, but he loved my mother and they had me."

As if Ryan were memorizing her face, his eyes never left
hers. "A very special relationship must have created you. I
understand about special. Last night was special for me."

She dropped her head, unable to respond to what she saw
in his eyes. She saw desire, but there was something more,
something incredibly open and honest. "It was pretty special
for me, too."

"You're blushing," he said. "I like that. Women don't
blush anymore. I think it's probably a good thing that Lottie
took your dad off. One look at us and he'd know how we
feel."

"No," she whispered. "I don't want it to be like that. Not
public. Obvious."

"You haven't told him?"

"No. I just said that we seemed to be connected. Everywhere I go, you're there. And that I was very confused."

"Still, he came?" That made him feel better. Not only was
Sunny taking their relationship seriously, but so was her father. So much so that he decided to come and check out the
man who was becoming connected to his daughter. He

wished the connection were literal. He was as hard as he'd been last night, and sooner or later, he had to be inside her.

"Sunny," he said, "let me hold you close, just for a minute."

She didn't move away. And when he pulled her against him, that part of him screaming for release nestled close to the place it ached to go. He groaned and put his hands beneath her bottom, pulling her even closer. "I want you so badly," he said. "Tell me you feel the same way." He rubbed himself against her and was rewarded with a tremble that caught in her breath and vibrated there. "Tell me!"

"Yes. Yes."

"How long is your father staying?"

"Until Wednesday, I think."

"Too long," Ryan growled. "I'll think of something."

"You'd better think of something quick," she managed to whisper. "I hear them coming."

Ryan let Sunny go, took several deep breaths and turned her toward the opposite wall in front of him. "And I bought these pieces by a local Atlanta artist several years ago at the Piedmont Arts Festival," he said. "Do you like them?"

"Where?" She couldn't see anything.

"They're miniatures. Let me switch on the light."

Seconds later, a small museum light was focused on three candy-bar size paintings. The sound of her father's laughter came closer. She looked, but a real viewing would have to come another day. "Very nice," she managed. Then, "Something smells good," she said, again. "What are we having?"

"Pork and beans and potatoes. I didn't know what your father would like."

"Pork and beans?" she said. "Really?"

Then he laughed as he realized how it sounded. "What, you think rich people don't eat pork and beans?"

"Ryan," Lottie called out, "come and meet Byron. No

wonder he's so romantic, his mother named him for Lord Byron, the poet."

Ryan took a hard look at Lottie's lipstick. It was a bit dull, but not smeared. Holding out his hand, he studied the Reverend Clary. His lips were clear but his face was flushed. He knew where Sunny learned to blush. He wondered if the father's and daughter's reasons were the same. "Good to meet you, sir."

Mr. Clary's handshake was firm. And his hands were rough. Whatever he was doing now, it was more physical than handling money and leading his flock.

"Any friend of my daughter's is a friend of mine" was the minister's reply. "Did I hear you say we're having pork and beans?"

Lottie let out a chortle. "Ryan cook pork and beans? I don't think so. Come on." She took Byron by the arm and pulled him into the kitchen. "What would you like to drink?"

"Whatever you have," he said, his attention now on Sunny. "I usually just drink water."

"We have wine, iced tea, soft drinks," Ryan said, making his way to the other side of the freestanding island where his stove top was located. "And I have coffee ready for later."

"But water is so...so plain. I know," Lottie exclaimed. "What about a nice wine cooler?" Without waiting for Byron's reply, she opened the refrigerator and pulled out two colorful bottles. "Raspberry or lemon?" She smiled and held up the red bottle. "Raspberry, I think. Are we ready to eat, Ryan?"

Ryan opened the oven and checked the contents. He nodded. "We're ready. The salad is already on the table and the cornbread is baking. By the time we're finished, the rest of the meal will be ready."

As if they'd always done it that way, Ryan put his hand on

Sunny's back and directed her into the dining area. Byron Clary didn't look at all bothered that he was escorting Lottie.

"This is some place you have here, Ryan," Byron said. "I'd get lost up here."

"It's pretty big for one man," he admitted. "But when I put up the building I thought I had to have it. It's a man's apartment, I guess, but lately, I've decided it's missing something."

"Nothing a woman's touch couldn't fix," Lottie said, sliding into her seat and beaming at her escort. "Tell me where you live, Byron."

"When Sunny was in college I sold the old house. I...I didn't need it anymore and she had stars in her eyes about her future. I knew she'd never come home again."

Ryan pulled out the chair across from Lottie and waited until Sunny was seated. "Pop thought I'd come to Atlanta or go to New Orleans right away. But I couldn't, not...then. Still, he's right, my career isn't in South Georgia. I know that now."

"So," Byron smiled and sat down, "now I live on the church grounds in a small house on the banks of the St. Mary's River. The house and the church are built of shale and river rock, over a hundred years old."

Lottie let out a pleased smile of satisfaction. "My house is over a hundred years old, too, Byron, at least the part of it that survived the War Between the States. Would you like to see it?"

"I'd love to."

"I'll take you—tomorrow."

"But, Pop, I promised my boss I'd bring you by the station tomorrow."

"So he can come to my house afterward. I'll pick you up," Lottie said. "You're gonna love my car."

Sunny was afraid to ask. But her father wasn't. "What kind of car do you have?"

"Don't laugh. It's a 1960 Cadillac convertible, pale blue with a white interior. Bought it new and paid for it myself. Stops traffic every time I drive it."

"She's right," Ryan murmured. "People get out of her way."

"Always wanted one," Byron admitted. "But it didn't seem right for a widower with a child. Stuck to sensible cars. But I'd love to see it. What time will I be through, Sunny?"

"I don't know what the schedule will be. Why don't we call Lottie from the station? Do you know where it is, Lottie?"

"Sure. Went down there once protesting some do-gooder's editorial about Lord Sin. Any idiot would know that the women were just enjoying fine art. That's not to say they wouldn't have run away with Sin if he'd been willing, but he was always careful about that. Their husbands ought to have appreciated what he did—not condemn it."

Sunny swallowed a cough. She'd intended to tell her father about Lord Sin, but she hadn't had a chance. She didn't know what he'd think of Lord Sin and Lottie. Though, after spending time in jail, he had to have seen a side of life he'd never come in contact with before.

"Who's Lord Sin?" he asked, his eyes flicking from Lottie to Sunny and back again. "Are you covering royalty now?"

This time Sunny couldn't hold back her laughter. She opened her mouth but no words came out. She glanced helplessly at Ryan.

"Lord Sin," Ryan explained, "is, or rather was, one of our more colorful local entertainers. He owned a series of clubs—"

"That's strip clubs," Lottie explained. "High-class adult entertainment clubs where you had to have a membership card to visit, except on Tuesday and Thursdays. That," she said quietly, as if waiting for his reaction, "was Ladies' Night."

"Lottie worked for him," Ryan said solemnly.

Sunny held her breath. She looked down at her salad bowl to find it was almost empty and she hadn't even known she was eating. What would her father say?

For a long dry-mouthed moment, he didn't say anything at all, then he began to chuckle. "Lottie, you were a stripper?"

Lottie looked hurt.

"I was. Are you going to hold that against me?"

Byron looked her straight in the eye and said, "Lottie, my girl, I have no intention of holding *that* against you. What happened to Lord Sin?"

"He retired and moved to the French Riviera," Lottie said, with a hard look at Ryan.

"I'll bet he is greatly missed," Byron said with a straight face. "And I look forward to seeing your house, Lottie."

With that, any concerns about bringing her father to dinner with Ryan and Lottie disappeared. When the pork and beans became medallions of pork and green beans, she allowed herself to smile. Ryan said nothing, but she felt his gaze on her, felt it burning a slice of her to a crisp. Here she'd brought her father to size up Ryan Malone, made out with Ryan in the hall and introduced her father to an ex-stripper, when all she'd wanted was her father's opinion of this man who'd steadily taken over her life. Instead of being the suspicious father, he seemed to like Ryan. He discussed baseball with Ryan and poetry with Lottie.

After they finished the fruit and ice cream, Sunny came to her feet. "Let me take the dishes to the kitchen for you, Ryan."

Ryan stood also. "Thank you. I'll get the coffee."

"No," Sunny said quickly. "Dad had a long drive up. I think we ought to go."

"Nonsense," her father countermanded. "I'd love coffee."

Sunny glared at her father. The lively expression in his usually solemn face said he was enjoying himself. She tried unsuccessfully to catch his eye, then gave up, stacked the plates and carried them to the kitchen. Ryan was filling two cups. "Give it up, Sunny, your dad's sunk. Haven't seen Lottie interested in a man since Ho left—if she really is. Let them have fun."

"Ho?"

"He owned the clubs where Lottie worked. She thought the sun rose and set on the old crook because he let her have her way. She looked after all the girls like a mother hen. Then Ho went back to San Francisco and married himself a bride straight from China. Lottie always swore he'd broken her heart."

"But Pop is...I mean, I don't think he's had much experience with women."

Ryan walked around the island and caught her hand. "And Lottie hasn't had much experience with men, not good men. Don't worry, Sunny. They'll be fine." He put one finger under her chin and lifted it, a sweet sober expression on his mouth. "And you'll be fine, once you get over being just a little jealous."

"I'm not jealous!" she said, twisting her face to the side.

"Of course not, and I don't want to kiss you either. Guess who's not telling the truth?"

Sunny let out the breath she felt as if she'd been holding for the better part of an hour and laid her cheek against his chest. "Ryan, I'm scared."

"Of what?"

"Of what I feel for you. I thought my dad would tell me to stop seeing you. But he seems to approve."

"Good," he said, lowering his lips to touch her hair. "I'm glad you have feelings for me. I wouldn't want to be feeling all this alone."

"What are we going to do?" she whispered.

"Forget about everything but us. Go where the feeling takes us. See where we end up."

"I can tell you where we're going to end up," Sunny said, looking at him again. "I'm going to be unemployed, Lottie's going to find herself barefoot and pregnant and Pop's going to be defrocked."

"Yeah!" Ryan said with a grin. "But ain't sinning going to be fun?"

10

THE RETURN TRAFFIC was light. On the way back to her apartment, her father was as jovial as she'd seen him in years.

"Nice people," Mr. Clary was saying. "I like your fella. He's been brought up well. He must have a nice family."

She hated to spoil his good mood but she didn't want her father to accept Ryan Malone so quickly. "Pop, he doesn't know who his father was and his mother died when he was very young."

"Who raised him?"

That stopped Sunny. "I don't know."

"Well, whoever it was, they did a mighty fine job. He has manners, a good business head on his shoulders—or he wouldn't live in a penthouse on top of his own office building—and from what Lottie tells me, he's generous with what he has. All in all, I approve."

"But, Pop, he's rich. He's one of Atlanta's most eligible bachelors. I can't believe he wants a country girl like me."

"Why not? Any man in his right mind would want you, Sunny. And I saw the way you looked at him."

Sunny grimaced. "Yeah, and I saw the way you looked at Lottie."

"Sara Frances!" Mr. Clary said, and tugged at a strand of her hair. "I know that people and the times have changed but if there's one thing I learned in prison, it's to appreciate the gifts that come to you while you have them. They may be gone and never come back. Keep trying to be the best person you can be but don't crush the feelings inside of you like I did. I'd love to see you find a good man and get married."

Sunny thought about what he was saying. She was being given a gift and she shouldn't turn it down. But was it love? And what would happen when Edward Hinton got through with them? "There's another thing I need your advice on, Pop."

"That's what I'm here for."

"I told you I covered a charity golf tournament yesterday. Ryan was playing. He invited me to have lunch with him and something happened. We were in the woods adjacent to the course when a bee flew down my shirt. I couldn't get it out."

"Oh, I'm sorry. Were you hurt?"

"I was stung, nothing serious. But Ryan had to get the bee. And someone took a picture of us with Ryan's hand inside my bra."

"Uh-oh! Someone, as in a fan, or someone who wants to cause you grief?"

"The latter, I'm afraid. The photograph was taken by a freelance newsman whose reputation has already gotten him fired from a television station and a newspaper in Atlanta. If those pictures reach the public, my credibility as an investigative reporter could be ruined. If nothing worse, I'll be a joke from now on."

"I see. What does Ryan think?"

Sunny took a deep breath. "He wanted to buy them back, the pictures and the negatives, to protect me."

"Good for him. That's what I'd expect. I feel better knowing you have someone looking after you up here. It's a different world from what you grew up in."

Not so very, she wanted to say. Instead, she asked, "Do you really like him?"

"I do. I like Lottie, too."

"We're a real pair. A country girl and a millionaire. A Baptist minister and an ex-burlesque star who is an assistant to a male stripper."

"Retired male stripper," her father corrected. "Living on the Riviera, according to Lottie."

"I'm not sure I believe that. A week ago he performed at the dedication of the building he donated to the Arts Council."

"And he's the story you're going after? The one Lottie and Ryan are helping you to get? Why do you need their help?"

"Because," Sunny said, "nobody else knows who he is."

Byron Clary laughed. "Son of a gun. He kept his identity secret. How'd he do that?"

"He wore a mask."

"If he didn't let anybody know who he was, he must have had a reason. I can see why that would interest you, but are you sure you want to reveal his secret?"

He was taking up for the man. Sunny was amazed. "You think I shouldn't?"

"I don't know. But when you track him down, I'd make certain I knew what I was doing before I told the world."

TED FIELDS AND THE REST of the staff welcomed her father. They shared coffee and doughnuts in the break room. Then Walt took him off to show him how videotape was edited. Sunny picked up her assignments for the day and was glad to see that none of them took her away from the station until an art show in the evening. "More fluff," she complained under her breath. When was Ted going to give her something with meat in it?

When Lottie showed up at noon, the entire male population of WTRU found an excuse to visit the parking lot to coo over Lottie's car.

Once they'd left, Sunny grabbed a sandwich and went to

work. If she stayed busy she wouldn't worry. Her father was over sixty; he could look after himself. She was the one who needed a keeper. When she looked down at her notepad all she'd written was *run away*.

Two rewritten stories from the news service and three voice-overs later and she found herself in the archives once more. If she could just get a line on Lord Sin she'd feel like she was accomplishing something.

The phone rang.

"Newsroom, Sunny Clary speaking."

"Phone booth. Edward Hinton speaking. We need to talk."

She didn't know why she hadn't expected it. It was logical. She was the one who'd refused to let Ryan pay; she was the one the blackmailer would work on. "Talk," she said.

"The pictures turned out great. Good clear shot of your...T-shirt, or where it would be normally."

"What do you want, Hinton?"

"I'm a reporter, Sunny. I always check my facts. I even checked on you. I don't want to hurt you, I know what that's like. I just want a job."

Her mind was racing. What should she do? "I don't do the hiring here. You know that."

"No, but you and your boyfriend have influence."

"Maybe I could get you an interview with Ted Fields. But the rest is up to you."

"Not good enough, babe. I was ambitious. I made mistakes, but I am a good reporter. WTRU is in the business of reporting the truth. If you need to know something, I can find it out."

She didn't like it, but at least it would buy her some time. If he failed, she hadn't lost anything. "Well," she said, planning her words carefully. "I have a project that might be right up your alley. Your reputation as a serious reporter is zilch. At the moment, so is mine. I'm willing to work with you on something that could get us both what we want. But if you let me down, my boss will ruin you."

"What do you need?"

"You've heard of Lord Sin?"

"The stripper? Sure. Everybody's heard of him."

"You help me find out who he really is. I'll give you half credit on the story and you give me the pictures you took of Malone and me in the woods."

"What's going to keep me from selling the story on Lord Sin and you, too?"

"Ryan Malone and your conscience and any hope you have for a future in television."

"And if I do what you want, you'll give me credit?"

"I will," she promised.

"You have a deal. What do you want me to do?"

"The labor department keeps a list of the strippers who worked for a man named Ho. This would have been fifteen years ago. I've been told that Lord Sin started out at one of the clubs as a janitor. Somebody had to have seen Lord Sin before he became Lord Sin. I would interview them myself but people are funny about talking to reporters. I want you to go."

"So, what am I, chopped liver?"

"It's not that, Hinton. They don't know you. You can use a different approach. I figure you probably stand a better chance of finding out what we want to know."

"And what are you going to do?"

"I'm going to work on Ryan Malone."

Her new partner laughed. "Yeah, I already saw how you managed that."

"Hinton, do you want to help me with this story or not?"

"I'll be in touch, partner," he said, and hung up.

The next phone call was from her father, telling her that

Lottie had made a seven o'clock dinner reservation at a restaurant owned by one of her old friends. He'd like to go—if Sunny didn't mind. "What time will you be home?" she asked, suddenly feeling like the parent.

She could hear him talking to Lottie before he answered, "Well, the restaurant is one of those places that serves courses, and she says it's pretty far out so we might be late. You sure you won't mind?"

She did, but since she had to cover the opening of the art show this evening, she could use the afternoon to contact Isabella. She had to know how to get to Lord Sin. Assuring her father she didn't mind, she hung up the phone. Her plan to have him size up Ryan Malone wasn't working out as she'd hoped anyway. He'd given Ryan his approval and now he seemed more interested in sizing up Lottie.

RYAN MALONE'S APPEARANCE at the show came as no surprise to Sunny. But the loss of electric power in the gallery moments later was a surprise. After thirty minutes of tinkering with fuses and wiring, the proprietor lit candles, held a solemn wake and invited the patrons to view the paintings by candlelight or come back the following night. "Well," Walt said, "that lets us out for tonight. I'm due at the Hawks' basketball game in exactly twenty minutes. You think Malone would give you a lift back to the station? Unless you'd rather come to the game."

"I'll be happy to take Sunny home," Malone said from the darkness behind them.

And that's how Sunny found herself in the big black sedan instead of the station van. "Do you know anything about wiring?" she asked suspiciously.

"Not enough to arrange that, but I would have, if I could. When is your dad due home?"

"I'm not sure. Lottie took him to some fancy restaurant owned by a friend."

Malone let out a chuckle and folded his hands beneath his chin in prayer. "Thank you, Lottie."

"What's so funny?" Sunny asked.

"I don't suppose he told you that the restaurant is in Chattanooga?"

"Chattanooga. You mean Tennessee? No, he didn't. He just said he'd be late."

"Well, Chattanooga is only an hour and a half north of Atlanta but, knowing Lottie, she probably didn't tell him. I'd say he'll be *very* late. How do you feel about leftovers?"

"I can't believe Lottie would do this. I can't believe my father would go along. He's over sixty. He's a minister."

"He's a man smitten, darling," Ryan said. "Trust me, being a minister doesn't mean he isn't still a man in love."

Sunny let out an aggravated sigh. "He can't be. He's been around Lottie twice. That's not love, that's pure lust."

Ryan turned his car into the parking deck under his building. "Well, I can't speak for your dad, but Lottie's never acted like this before. She's ready to give up her Victorian cottage for a house on a churchyard by the river."

That left Sunny speechless. Lottie as a minister's wife?

The car came to a stop and Ryan slid out and opened Sunny's door. "Come on, darling, let's raid the icebox."

Sunny was in the elevator when she realized what she was doing. "Wait. What are we doing here?"

"I'm going to feed you," Ryan said.

The elevator opened to his foyer.

"But I'm not hungry," Sunny glanced at her watch. What on earth was wrong with her? Instead of concentrating on her future she was worrying about her father. And putting herself in a risky situation in the meantime. "Can we just...talk?"

"Talk? Yes. I think we can find something to talk about," he said, opening the door and drawing Sunny inside and into his arms. He pulled her close and fitted his body into all the places it was meant to fit. "Later."

"Ryan..." She forgot what she intended to say. She forgot her story. She forgot Lord Sin. In the space of a moment her heart was in her throat, tight from wanting this man. She'd known this had to happen, she just hadn't expected it so soon. She was through fooling herself; she wanted him—whatever the cost. She touched his face, his hair, pulling him down so that she could kiss him. Lord Sin could wait. "There's no future to this," she said, licking her lips. "We both understand that."

"I know you're just interested in today. That's what you told me when we first met. I'm the one who does the long-range planning. You're just interested in the now. Well, now, Sunny Clary. I've told you every way I know how that I'm...I'm interested in you. What do you say? Tell the truth, Miss Sunny Clary of WTRU News."

"I say, where's the bedroom, Malone? I want to see your sheets."

Ryan let out a small silent thank-you. Then he kissed her, lifted her into his arms and made his way through the half-dark room, down the corridor and into the bedroom. He only turned on a small light by the bed. More light could spook her. Then he let her down, kissing her over and over again as he undressed her.

"Look at me, Sunny," he finally said.

"No. For the first time in my life, I don't want anything to be real," she protested. "With my eyes closed, it's a dream."

"This isn't one of Lord Sin's fantasies, dammit, Sunny. This is real. Besides, you can see my sheets," he said.

"Sheets?" Sunny opened her eyes. They were in Ryan's bedroom, standing beside a bed as big as a putting green.

He'd pulled back the comforter, exposing white satin sheets. Her breath caught. "Satin sheets? Sinful, yes. But they don't seem like you, Malone."

"They aren't me. They're for you, Sunny. This is the way I saw you in my imagination that first night, totally nude with your hair tousled across white satin sheets."

"Then you're in big trouble."

His forehead furrowed. "Trouble?"

"Yes. You've taken off all my clothes and you're still wearing yours."

"We can take care of that," he said. Slowly and deliberately, he discarded his shirt and trousers, his eyes planted fiercely on her. He continued to talk as if he were afraid she'd turn and run away if he hushed.

"Why? Why me?" Her voice was hoarse and so low that she could barely hear it. "I know there have been other women."

"You're the first one who mattered."

Sunny didn't know what to say. Until now she'd only looked at his face, at hungry eyes that churned like a black ocean in a storm. Now she allowed her gaze to wander lower, across his chest, firm, muscular and sprinkled with silky dark hair. He stood, his legs apart, his lower body gloriously nude. He made no apology for his erection and she had no words to describe the thrumming of her pulse at the sight of it.

Finally, she raised her eyes to his, managed a quick grin and whispered, "No underwear?"

"I had hopes. Let me love you, Sunny?"

She gave him the only answer she could. "Yes."

He scooped her up and fell into bed, supporting himself with his elbows as he covered her. "I've wanted this from the first moment I saw you. You've driven me crazy with your taunts."

"Taunts?" Her voice was one of disbelief.

"You told Lord Sin that you couldn't be seduced just by a voice and you challenged him to do better than that. You seemed so taken with him. I'll admit it, I was jealous."

"He's very good at seduction, Ryan, but it isn't Lord Sin whose lips set me on fire, Ryan Malone. It's you."

This time when he kissed her, she held nothing back. For the first time in her life she gave as much as she got, touching, tasting, feeling the warm contact of their skin that felt like velvet against velvet. She unleashed all the passion that had been building up since that first night, letting the emotion fuel her body and her heart. Everything hurt so good, so good that she never wanted it to end.

She was in his arms, then he was over her, pressing against her, moving so slowly that she wanted to scream, "Hurry! Hurry!"

"Not yet," he answered and she hadn't known that she'd spoken aloud.

His mouth was all over her. She could feel his hot breath, hear the ragged inhaling and exhaling as he seemed intent on driving her slowly mad. There was nothing shy about her as she caught his head between her hands and forced him upward, forced him to kiss her, forced him on top. Spreading her legs she let go of his thick dark hair and caught his body, holding it so that he was rubbing against the pool of slick moisture that suddenly allowed him inside.

"Oh!" he moaned, and plunged deeper. Then jerked back, pulling himself out. "Dammit, Sunny, I haven't—stop!"

She reached between them and took him into her hand. "I'm here in your bed and I want you to make love to me, Malone. Isn't this what you wanted?"

He pushed her hand away while he fumbled beneath the pillow, opened the packet and pulled its contents over his own throbbing need.

"It is, my lady of green fire," he murmured as he took in a deep calming breath. "I won't walk away this time, Sunny."

"I don't want you to, Ryan."

But he wasn't ready yet. Carefully pressing himself against her, he caught her legs and pressed them together. "Don't move." He slid his hands upward, across her sides to her breasts, splaying his fingers to cover her nipples, that now hurt with need. Thin, long and tapered, his fingertips were as tan as her own sun-kissed color. She looked at those hands and smiled. They felt right, as if she'd always known them. Then he began to move against her once more. Slowly, slipping inside the sanctuary anxious to be filled, then out again, teasing her, promising, driving her even wilder. As he moved, she felt the hair on his chest skim her nipples. She groaned.

At that moment he plunged inside her and she felt the earth turn and her release overwhelmed her. And then, as he shuddered she knew. This wasn't sex. This was a binding of two souls, two lovers who belonged together.

After the last ultimate ripple subsided, they lay together, still joined. His face was buried in her neck, his hot, ragged breath slowing. He let go of her hips, moving his hands to catch her own and lacing his fingers through hers. She nuzzled his hair with her chin and felt a wave of dizziness sweep over her. She wanted to laugh. To cry. To open the penthouse window and fly through the night sky. She wanted to do this every night for the rest of her life and longer.

And then he raised his head and the look in his eyes pierced her very being. There was happiness and pain and uncertainty. The great Ryan Malone was as vulnerable now as she was and they both understood that she knew it.

"Sunny...I—"

"It's all right, Ryan," she whispered. "I know we're in your bed. You can't come up with some kind of business deal that demands your leaving. So you already have my excuse. I have to leave."

He stretched up, kissed her gently. "I'm not going anywhere and neither are you."

"Don't make me any promises you don't intend to keep, Ryan."

"I won't."

He covered her mouth with his own and with little persuasion she gave herself to him. For most of the night, they made love, slept, then made love again. Long after Sunny fell into sated sleep, he lay and watched her. He'd never understood about love before, never considered what it meant. But now he did. Loving meant being close, caring about what a person felt and needed. Wanting always to be with them.

It was almost dawn when Ryan touched Sunny on her shoulder and wakened her. "I think we'd better get you home, darling. I mean if it were up to me, I'd never let you go but I don't want your father to have me arrested."

Sunny came awake. "Oh, Ryan, you shouldn't have let me sleep. I wanted to talk to you."

But Ryan was already dressed. He'd gathered up Sunny's clothing and stood back while she tugged them on. A rough brushing of her hair and she was on her way, her Prince Charming bent on protecting her reputation, a reputation she'd smeared long ago. He put his arm around her and kissed her again.

Accept the gifts you are given, she told herself all the way home. They may only come once. Lord Sin might be her future, but Ryan Malone was her glorious present.

"I want to talk to you, Sunny," Ryan said as they pulled up in the drive. "But not now. Sometimes a good thing is ruined when you talk about it. Let's wait."

Sunny nodded, too happy to argue. At the top of the stairs she pushed open the door and paused, waiting to hear her father's voice. After a few moments, she realized that she was only hearing silence. "Pop?"

Nothing.

She switched on the light. The couch was empty. The bed was empty. "He isn't home," Sunny said. "My father has stayed out all night with a woman."

"Don't worry," Ryan said, "Lottie will make an honest man of him, or she'll answer to me."

11

BYRON CLARY HAD CALLED and left a message on her answering machine. "Don't wait up, Sara Frances. Lottie and I are having so much fun we've decided to stay over. We'll be home tomorrow."

"Be home tomorrow? My father leaves me a message that he's having so much fun he's not coming home? I don't believe it."

Ryan didn't know what to say. If he had Lottie here, he'd personally strangle her. For most of his life, he'd loved all her wild Auntie Mame notions but Byron Clary wouldn't have a clue how to deal with her. For all he knew, they could be halfway to Maui. And Sunny was obviously worried.

"What are they doing, to have so much fun?" Sunny asked.

Ryan smothered a smile. "I don't think I want to answer that," he said. "But if it would make you feel any better, I'll give Lottie's friend at the restaurant a call."

"Will you?" She didn't know what that would tell her, but at least it was something.

Ryan glanced at his watch. "It might be a bit early, or late, depending on how you look at it. Why don't we get some breakfast and give him time to get up, then I'll call? Sunny?" He caught her hand and pulled her close. "Don't worry. Your father can take care of himself. Trust me, darling. They'll be fine."

Darling. She allowed herself to lean against him. First her mother had died. Then, her father had gone to jail. Though she was an adult when that happened, she'd missed him so badly. Now he was finding a new life for himself and she was jealous. Suddenly, she felt foolish. For the first time in so long, she had someone strong enough for her to lean on. It felt good. Ryan was right. But it was happening too fast. "I do trust you. And for me, last night was very special but I need to get ready to go to work now, Ryan. You go home and call Lottie's friend, then call me later at the station."

She let Ryan kiss her, held him tight for a moment, then watched as he drove away, a frown of concern marring his strong face. It was too early for work. They both knew it, but she needed space, time to think, time to gather herself. She needed a shower and a clear head, not swirling with memories of the night before. Everything had changed.

And she didn't know where she was headed.

Finally, she dressed, arriving at the station long before the day crew. If she could find Lord Sin, one of her problems would be solved. Work had always been the answer when she'd been troubled and she fell back on that to keep from thinking about Ryan. She'd tried to contact Isabella without success, so now she turned to the archives for information about Lord Sin. After an hour of searching in vain, she stopped for coffee and a sweet roll from the machine, then headed back to her desk. It was amazing that the man could have been so successful and remained a mystery. But he had.

Without an immediate assignment to carry out, her mind flew back to Ryan Malone. She forced herself to focus on the man, not the lover. It seemed ironic that the moment Lord Sin retired from performing, Ryan began his meteoric rise to riches. He joined the Chamber of Commerce and bought his first office building. In the five years since, that building had become the flagship, the basis for the real estate holdings he'd amassed. She saw picture after picture of him, always with a beautiful woman at his elbow, rarely the same one.

Temporary was all she could expect. She'd known that from the beginning. It hadn't mattered before but all that had changed now. He told her this relationship was different, that she'd have to trust him. But it was hard. She was falling in love with Ryan Malone and she didn't know what she'd do when he left her.

Her phone rang.

"Newsroom, Sunny Clary speaking."

"Get ready to write your story, Sunny. I think I have something."

It was Edward Hinton. "What? Tell me."

"I have a high school yearbook with a picture. One of the dancers had it. I think she was a little in love with your boy. Held on to it all this time. You're going to be a happy camper."

Her heart began to race. "Bring it over," she said.

"No. You meet me for lunch." He sounded smug. "You're buying."

"Where?"

"At Aggie's Diner. It's in the next block, toward town. I'll be waiting."

The next call was from Ryan. "They stayed at the Chattanooga Choo Choo." There was a long pause. "Separate rooms, Sunny. They left about an hour ago. Should be home about lunchtime. I told you they'd be all right."

"I know you did. Thank you."

"Want me to pick you up, take you and your dad to lunch?"

"No. I have an assignment."

"Anything important?"

She should tell him about Hinton. It would be the smart

thing to do, but this was her work, her future and something made her hold back. "No. Just routine."

She hung up the phone, picked up her purse and left. But her heart wasn't racing anymore; it felt tight and full. Her father would be back soon. Ryan Malone was hers for another ten days, give or take a couple—she wasn't fooling herself about that—and she was on the verge of her big story, the story that would earn her the credibility she needed. It all depended on how well she handled Edward Hinton.

He'd taken a booth in the corner. As she entered the diner he looked up and signaled with a nod of his head. "Sit down," he said. "You want to order?"

"Just bring me a glass of iced tea," she said to the waitress, dismissing her quickly and turning to Edward. "Show me."

He twisted the book lying on the table between them, the North Atlanta High School annual, *The Messenger*. "You know I could do this by myself," he said.

"I know. But you won't. We have a deal. You and I will write this story, together. We both need this, Edward. Don't mess it up."

He nodded, still suspicious, but willing to go along for the moment. "You think Ted will go for this?"

She nodded, hoping she was right. "Now show me."

He opened the yearbook and pointed. "This is Lord Sin."

The man—no, the boy—in the colored portrait was a tawny-haired stallion, dramatic, classically beautiful. She stared at him for a long time, then raised her eyes in question.

"Yep," Edward said. "He's the guy."

She let her gaze fall lower to the name, Jackson Lewis "Jack" Ivy. Sunny studied the picture. There was something vaguely familiar about him but she didn't recognize the face.

Edward gave her a smirking look. "You don't recognize that name, Jackson Lewis? Old Atlanta money. Politician.

Never married, but fathered a child that ended up in an ugly paternity suit. The girl was an intern in his father's office at the capital. She was studying law, had big plans until Jackson promised her the moon, then deserted her—in public. That was before DNA testing. She sued him and lost, but according to my source Jackson was your boy's father and the family couldn't stop her from calling her son by his father's given name."

"Where'd the Ivy come from?"

"Ivy was apparently her name."

"Where is Jackson Lewis now?"

"Dead. Killed himself in a car wreck when little Jack was only three years old. Don't know how our Jack came to work for one of Ho's clubs when he was just a kid. But the dancers adopted him and eventually he took the name Lord Sin and Jack Ivy went underground."

Sunny frowned. "So why hasn't the yearbook turned up before now? I don't know. This just seems a little too convenient. We need to identify Lord Sin and you turn up not only a face but a name."

"Hey, I do good work," Edward said. "Is it enough for a story? The old broad I got this from wouldn't agree to an interview. She told me to talk to the mystery man's manager, a woman named—"

"I know, Lottie Lamour."

"That's her. When do you want to go talk to her?"

"Give me your number. Let me do a little research on Jack Ivy and talk to Ted. I'll call you. In the meantime, stay away from Lottie."

It was Edward's turn to frown. "You wouldn't be planning to cut me out, would you? Remember, I still have the pictures from the golf tournament."

"I'm aware of that. If you sell the pictures, you sell them. That doesn't change our agreement. I keep my word."

Sunny wrote down Edward's number, picked up the year-book and the ticket for his lunch. He was tearing into a hamburger with all the trimmings when she left. With most of her lunch hour left, she swung by her apartment to find her father asleep on the couch. At her entrance, he sat up, smiling.

"Morning, Sara Frances. You're looking ravishing this morning."

"Pop, I'm glad you're home. I was...a little worried about you last night."

He looked surprised. "You were worried about me, a sixty-three-year-old man who is a minister?"

"I was. Pop, you don't understand. You haven't had much experience with women like Lottie. She's—different."

"You got that right. I like her—a lot. I haven't felt so alive in years."

Sunny frowned. How did a daughter talk to her father about his having a midlife crisis? Did she even have the right? "Look," she finally said, "I have to get back to work, but we'll talk about this tonight. I love you and I just don't want you to be hurt."

"I wish we could, sweetheart, but I have to get back. My assistant called a little while ago. We lost Jed Lake yesterday. Have to get home to preach the funeral. I was just catching a quick nap before I started the drive back." He laughed. "Didn't get much sleep last night."

"But Pop—"

"Oh, about your young man. I had a long talk with Lottie about him. He's okay. I'd say you ought to get to know him better." He stopped and gave her a long, troubled look. "Sunny, I love you. I never told you that very often, but I do. I wasn't much of a father to you, either. I'm sorry. When your mother died, I was lost. I know what being alone can do to a person. I'm thinking that's not good."

"But Pop—" she began again, ready to argue. She'd had a father and that was more than a lot of girls. And if he had been distant, so had she. But she'd always known that he loved her, in his own way.

"Don't be such a worrywart, Sara Frances. Remember what I said. We only get so many gifts. I wasted a lot of years. Don't waste yours. Life's a bowl of cherries," he added as he disappeared into the bathroom and turned on the shower, whistling merrily. "And the Lord sent us cherries to be eaten."

His poetry might be lousy, but all the way back to the station Sunny heard the sound of her father whistling. A long time had passed since she'd heard it. She wanted him to be happy, didn't she? Was it him she was worried about, or her?

The afternoon schedule was slow. Ted had a day off. Sunny was disappointed. She'd have to wait until tomorrow to discuss what she'd learned about Lord Sin. In the meantime, the archives revealed no information about Jackson Lewis Ivy but she did learn about the man who was supposed to be his father, Jackson Lewis. Lewis was a classic underachiever. He was a stereotypical rich kid with a spotty school record which indicated that his failure to graduate was due to a poor attitude and sheer laziness. He'd started out in the family business but after a few years received an appointment to fulfill the term of a county commissioner who died in office. An apparent charge of misuse of the county expense account was hushed up and Jackson went back to the family business. Finally, with a war chest that dwarfed all the other candidates, he ran for state representative from his district and was elected.

His career seemed less than illustrious, ending in the automobile wreck that claimed his life. There was no record of a marriage, a wife or a child, legitimate or otherwise. If the boy in the annual was Jackson's son, he'd apparently never enjoyed any of the benefits. From what she'd read of Jackson senior, it was just as well.

Finally, she typed up her notes. There was a story here, at least the beginning of one. She'd have to talk to Lottie again. After what had happened with Ryan, then her father, she wasn't certain she wanted to face the woman who had so much influence over both. Still, it had to be done. She was a reporter and she couldn't let her personal life interfere with her job. A vow was a vow and she'd made one never to give up again, even if it meant putting herself at risk.

She picked up the phone and dialed Lottie's number.

RYAN HAD OCCUPIED HIMSELF for most of the day with making the final arrangements for the dedication for the hospital wing, but his mind had often dwelled on Sunny. He'd finally found a woman he really cared for. One who was stubborn, compassionate and totally unimpressed with his wealth. Everything he'd worked for was in place. Why then was he nagged by such doubts? Something was wrong. He just couldn't figure out what it was.

Then the phone rang. Lottie's worried voice put a face on his doubt. "Ryan, she's found the yearbook."

"Well, that's what we wanted, isn't it?"

"That's what you wanted. I'm not sure it was the right thing to do. We should have just told her Lord Sin had retired to the Riviera like we'd planned and let it go at that."

"Wouldn't have worked, Lottie. She's a reporter. She wouldn't have given up."

"And you think she will now?"

"Yes. We've given her something to investigate, a trail to follow. When she comes to you, you identify Jackson Ivy as Lord Sin. Answer her questions. She'll be able to trace his real estate holdings to the Riviera and once the AP news photo of Jack opening his restaurant comes to the station, she'll have her story."

"I don't like it, Ryan. In the beginning you said something about telling her the truth. I think you should. If what her daddy told me about Sunny is true, I think she'd understand. She isn't the bright-eyed, tell-the-truth-at-any-cost person she once was either."

"Sunny never had anything to hide. She was never a stripper," Ryan said.

"No, more's the pity," Lottie said. "Can you imagine Lord Sin and Sunny Clary performing together? We'd have had to keep the cops from arresting you. Sure you don't want to go back to work?"

"The only stripping I'll ever do again will be private," Ryan said, remembering last night, "very private."

SUNNY HAD MADE ONE wrong turn on the way to Lottie's house. Asking Ryan to accompany her had crossed her mind but she'd rejected that idea as being distracting at a time when she needed all her wits about her.

Lottie let her in and offered her tea. Sunny shook her head and went right to the point. "I'd like you to look at this high school yearbook, Lottie, and tell me if you know this man?"

She flipped open the pages and pushed it over to Lottie who took a deep breath and looked down.

After a long minute she nodded. "Yes, that's my beautiful Sin."

"And his name is Jackson Lewis Ivy?"

"That was the name his mother gave him. Sin never used it. If the man who was his father wouldn't give him his name, Sin didn't want it."

"How'd he get the name Sin?"

"Well," she smiled and rolled her eyes, "when he first came to the house, he thought it was a restaurant. We'd run an ad for a part-time janitor. When I saw him, I said it would be a sin to give a handsome boy like him a job emptying the trash. He laughed and blinked those big eyes at the girls and they all agreed that it would be a sin to hide him. So, we called him Sin. Then Ho sold the club and, later, when the new owner came in, Sin lied about his age and put together an act. I helped him change his appearance and gave him a royal title. Jackson Lewis Ivy disappeared forever when Lord Sin began to dance."

"Why didn't you tell me this before? Why was it so important to keep it a secret?"

"Because when Sin was in high school, his father's family finally contacted the foster parents he lived with. They wanted to make amends for treating Sin's mother so badly. What they really wanted was their son back. But it was too late. Jackson Ivy had run away from the foster home where he was living and vanished. If his mother wasn't good enough for the Lewises, he wanted no part of them. He made me promise to keep his secret. I have ever since. Until now."

"How sad. And where is Jack?"

"Lord Sin did very well, as you know. He saved his money, invested it and made a fortune. Finally, he retired and moved to the Riviera where people don't care who you were, only what you've got. Jack Ivy owns a mansion on the beach and a restaurant called Ivy's which is the hottest thing going. So, now you have your story. Write it up and let the mystery of Lord Sin die a natural death."

"I suppose," Sunny said. Now that she knew the truth, it seemed so sad. At least she had information that could be verified. And once she'd told Ted, she would have earned her right to pick her assignments. Gathering up the annual, she started toward the door.

"By the way, Sunny," Lottie said softly, "I really like your dad. He's the kind of man any woman would want. Why hasn't he married since your mom died?"

Lottie's question startled Sunny. "My mother was such a big part of my daddy's life. When she died, he just filled that space with work. Then he had a little bad luck."

"Yeah, he told me about being framed. If it had been me, when I got out I'd have done bodily harm to the real bad guy. But Byron said a higher power already had."

Sunny nodded. "He was killed in a boating accident while Pop was in jail."

"I know. It's kinda nice having a friend upstairs who has pull. He's made me think about things I haven't thought about in years."

Sunny cut her gaze back to Lottie. "Like what?"

"Like sharing. Like discovering new things. Like opening myself to possibilities. I hope you don't mind, Sunny, but I intend to see your father again."

"You know he's a preacher in a church too poor to support a full-time man. I doubt they have more than twenty-five members."

"You're out of date, Sunny," she said with a laugh. "Your father is gathering souls with a vengeance. The church is up to fifty members now and growing. Besides, I don't need a man with money, I have a pot full. I just need something or *somebody* to spend it on. This morning I'm going shopping for a church organ. Byron's going to be surprised when he finds out I can play a mean piano. An organ ought not to be too hard to learn."

SUNNY WAS ON HER WAY HOME when she turned back to the station and the archives. Something wasn't right. The story was there, the explanation and enough proof to make her think that she was on the right track. But there was some little sixth sense that was nagging at her.

As she turned into the parking lot, she was followed by a car that parked beside her. Ted got out. "You're working late," he said.

"Just doing a little research," she said. "Thought you were off today."

"Today, not tonight. What about you?" Ted asked. "What are you doing here?"

"I'd like to talk to you about that. Do you have a few minutes?"

"Sure. Come on in."

Sunny followed him into his office and took the seat across from Ted's desk. "I've found Lord Sin," she said.

His look of surprise was even bigger than she'd expected. "You don't look too excited about it," he commented as he slid out of his jacket and hung it on a rack by the door. "Something wrong?"

"I'm not sure. Look at this picture and tell me what you think." She opened the annual and pointed at the picture of Jack Ivy.

"Good-looking kid" was Ted's comment. "Don't understand why he'd want to hide all that blond hair and those blue eyes under a mask."

"I guess that's what's bothering me. Does he look familiar to you?"

"Vaguely, maybe. But you saw him dance, you ought to know."

"Lord Sin's hair was the same blond and his eyes were the same blue."

"Well, then..." Ted said.

Sunny gave him the story that Lottie had told. "I just wish there was some way we could verify that Jack Ivy actually owns a restaurant and a beachfront mansion on the Riviera."

"Well—" he thought a minute "—there ought to be somebody who could tell us. I have a couple of friends who work with the foreign press. Let me make a few inquiries."

Those were the kind of contacts Sunny needed to develop but that would come later. For now, she felt better. She stood up and smiled. "Thanks, Ted. I'll let you get back to work now. See you tomorrow."

"Sunny." His voice stopped her at the door. "Good work. We'll talk tomorrow about your next assignment. You've earned something with some teeth."

"Good. By the way," she called out, "I promised Edward Hinton he'd get some credit on the story. I couldn't have done it without him."

"What?" Ted's roar followed her across the newsroom. "Who gave you the authority to promise anything? Sunny?"

But Sunny kept going. She'd done it. Ted was going to let her do something meaningful. This would mean that Edward wouldn't sell the photographs of Ryan touching her breasts and she'd be perceived as a serious journalist. Everything was going to work out. Suddenly she was in a hurry to get home. Suppose Ryan had tried to call?

He had. He'd left a message on her answering machine that some business in South Georgia had come up. He'd call her tomorrow. "The dedication of the children's hospital wing at Doctor's Hospital takes place Wednesday afternoon. I hope you'll be the one they send."

Sunny thought about Ted's promise and groaned. "Probably," she said, answering the machine rather than the man. "I'm the Good-News Girl, aren't I? But that is about to change."

Her carriage house apartment seemed very quiet. When the doorbell rang later, she dashed to answer, hoping that Ryan's trip had been canceled. Instead, a messenger handed her a special delivery package. "Sign here, please," he said, then disappeared into the darkness. Locking the door behind him, she carried the package inside and ripped open the other paper. Inside were two large picture puzzles—and a note. "Until we see these in person, this will have to do."

She was holding The Bridge of Sighs in Vienna and a street scene of Paris in the rain. "Oh, Ryan," she whispered. "What am I going to do with you?" Then, after a moment, she added, "And what am I going to do without you, when you get tired of me?"

Later, in bed, she tossed and turned, unable to sleep, missing Ryan's arms around her, feeling his lips on hers. She'd never minded being alone before. The problem with loving someone was dealing with the loss when it was over. Losing Ryan Malone was going to be rough. She didn't know if she could do it. Finally, she got up and switched on Lord Sin's tape. She might as well finish it. She couldn't be still anyway.

This time she stopped the tape on a close-up and studied his face. Though it was masked and the lighting was strange, she could clearly see his eyes and his mass of golden hair, straight and flowing this time. It was the hair that bothered her. Why would a man who kept his identity a secret wear a hairstyle that could never be disguised? It made no sense. Yet, that's what he'd done. The picture in the yearbook confirmed he'd worn it from the start.

As the tape played, she soon got caught up in his dancing, watching the sensual way he was able to make love to a woman who wasn't there. His voice, always an intimate whisper and filled with emotion, seemed directed at her. "You're the woman I've waited for, longed for. You've made me feel your hot breath, and your heart race. You are a part of me. Together, we have worlds to travel and wonders to see."

The tape ended. The phone rang.

"Hello, darling," Ryan's husky voice said. "Are you missing me?"

The racing heart Lord Sin just talked about was nothing compared to Sunny's. The sound of Ryan's voice turned up her temperature to blistering. "I thought for a moment you were Lord Sin."

There was a silence. "Do I sound like him?"

"Only because I was watching his video. I don't understand the man. His blue eyes and blond hair were so spectacular. But it was his voice. He always whispered. He couldn't have done that without the microphone. And it disguised his real speaking voice."

"You sound a little breathless. I wish I were there."

"I am and I wish you were, too." She leaned back against her pillow and moved her legs and remembered Ryan's satin sheets. "What would you do?"

Once he'd told her, Sunny groaned aloud, threw off the covers and walked to the window, picturing them naked and tangled in the sheets. *How long will it take you to get here?* she wanted to ask. But that was a fantasy; that's all it could be.

"Did you get my present?"

"I did. Thank you. I've always wanted to travel. Have you been to Venice?"

"Not with you," he said. "But we'll go. Together, we have worlds to travel and wonders to see," he said. "For now, look at the canal and see us there. In the moonlight, in a gondola. See you in my arms. See me kissing you. Good night, Sunny."

After she hung up she realized that she hadn't told him she knew the truth about the mystery man.

12

WEDNESDAY MORNING Ted's friend with the Associated Press faxed a copy of a shot of the opening of Ivy's Restaurant on the Riviera. The view of the new owner was slightly blurred but even to Sunny, it was clear that the man welcoming the Princess of Monaco was Lord Sin, now known as Jack Ivy. There was also a smaller photo, an overhead view of an estate, identified as the new digs of the Riviera's newest multimillionaire.

"Looks like you did it," Ted said. "Here's your proof. But you've put me in an awkward position with Edward Hinton. I talked to him. I told him that once he hands over the photos of you and Malone, he'll get half credit on the story. But that doesn't mean he's going to join our staff."

"He doesn't have to. I never said you'd do that. I just hope he's learned his lesson. If he's taken seriously, he'll be able to do some more freelance work. But, Ted, if he does sell my photo, it won't be the end of the world."

"I hope not. In the meantime, how about one last good-news assignment?"

"I know," she said, shaking her head. "Cover the opening of the children's wing in the hospital this afternoon."

"Yep, and starting Monday, you get city hall."

That brought Sunny out of her chair. "City hall?" She all but jumped across the desk and threw herself into the news director's arms.

"You heard me. You're getting what you wanted, kid, a

chance to be an investigative reporter in the big city of Atlanta. You earned it."

She had. She'd proved to the world that she could get her story and that she wouldn't be silenced again—ever. And this time the truth didn't hurt anyone. "Thanks, Ted," she said and moved toward the door.

"Hey, Sunny, there's still one more thing I want from you."

She stopped. "What?"

"The interview with Ryan Malone you promised me."

She nodded. With any luck, she might get that interview this afternoon. At any rate, she'd get a story.

The wind was brisk but the sun was bright. The afternoon was turning out to be one of those rare days that comes just before winter gives its last gasp. She met up with Walt at the van and they headed toward the hospital. A respectable crowd had gathered in front of a temporary platform outside the shiny new hospital wing. Behind the podium she could see a structure shrouded with a soft blue cover. On the platform several people were already seated. Sunny watched as Anne Kelly approached her.

"Sunny," she called out, "I was hoping they'd send you. Would you like to meet Mr. Roberts, the hospital administrator?"

"Uh, sure, thanks." Sunny allowed herself to be drawn to the platform, indicating to Walt that he should tape. "Mr. Roberts, Sunny Clary, WTRU. I've read your brochure. This is certainly an impressive facility. Can you tell our television audience what it means to the children of Atlanta?"

"Indeed I can. As of today, no child will be refused emergency treatment because they can't pay for it. We can't solve all their problems, at least not yet, but as of today, we have the finest trauma staff in the south. Accident victims, burns, severe injury, disease, if we can't treat it, at least we can stabilize until the child can be moved."

"That's pretty impressive."

"And it's all thanks to the man headed this way, Ryan Malone," the administrator said.

Sunny turned, her microphone still in hand.

"Hello, Sunny," Ryan said. "We're so glad you're here to cover our dedication of the new wing." He was being very formal today. That was good. Their relationship had been far too lax in public.

At that moment Mr. Roberts stepped to the microphone and began. "Good afternoon." He gave a short history of the new facility and talked about the future plans to expand the wing to include the prenatal care of women, then said, "I'd like to welcome you and ask you to help me welcome a very special guest, Callie Ferguson."

The crowd's attention was directed to a wheelchair being rolled toward the platform. In the chair was a tiny, pale little girl wearing an absurd straw hat with pink roses. At the steps Ryan held out his arms. Weakly, the child raised her arms and gave him a sweet smile. Holding her carefully, he climbed to the podium and moved to the mike.

"I'm Ryan Malone and this is Callie, the very first patient to be treated in the children's wing. She is five years old and is recovering from the removal of a brain tumor." He lowered his voice to a gentle whisper. "Callie is what this is all about, Callie and all the children like her who need someone to care about them. Callie, will you help me show the folks our memorial?"

Ryan wrapped the cord around her hand and together they tugged. Like a ship on the ocean, the blue fabric caught the wind and billowed away. Beneath its cover was a white winged creature, a marble angel with a peaceful smile.

"This angel will watch over the children inside. The wing

and this sculpture are memorials to my mother, Helen. They will remind us all that someone cares."

Someone cares. Sunny felt a lump in her throat. Ryan's love for children had come through the night of the awards dinner. But it wasn't just children he cared for. He looked after Isabella and others who needed someone to care. Her heart swelled. This was a good man who did good things in the name of truth and commitment.

Ryan gave the child a kiss and gently returned her to her chair. After the ceremony, the group moved inside to tour the hospital. Sunny and Walt returned to the station, both filled with emotion from what they'd seen. Viewing the video, Sunny composed her story. When Walt cut to the plate at the base of the statue she stopped the tape, enlarging the inscription.

In memory of Helen Ivy Malone
by her son, Ryan

Helen Ivy? *Ivy?* The next frame showed Ryan, recorded his whispered voice and the tender kiss he gave Callie. He was looking straight at the camera, almost as if his eyes were focused on the lens. She'd heard that whisper before. She'd seen those eyes before, eyes that she'd thought were blue. She reeled. Her head spun as understanding washed over her like a cold wind. The blond hair was meant to be a distraction all along. Lord Sin was, and had always been, a black-haired rogue. He had to have been wearing blue contact lenses.

And he'd whispered. The voice on the tape had said, "We have worlds to travel and wonders to see," the same words Ryan had used on the phone last night. She even remembered him quoting words she'd spoken to Lord Sin, but she hadn't clued in at the time. Now it all fit together.

Ryan Malone was Lord Sin. There couldn't be another answer. That explained his close association with Lottie, with Isabella. The fact that he suddenly appeared at the same time Lord Sin retired. That's why she'd been so attracted to them both. Why hadn't he told her? The only answer was manipulation and seduction; Ryan Malone had lied to her and everyone else from the beginning.

Obviously he was ashamed of how he'd made his money. Obviously, too, he wanted no connection to his real father's family. He'd done everything he could to protect his identity, even going so far as creating a retirement for Lord Sin in a place where the local people wouldn't be likely to challenge his past. At the same time, he'd built a new persona, one of wealth and power. Knowing that, his relationship with a woman determined to be an investigative reporter was taking a real risk. Why?

Of course. How stupid could she have been? She, the darling of Atlanta's WTRU, the Good-News Girl, was to be his final protection. Everything he'd done had been to that end. He'd set out to use her from the beginning, use her to tell Lord Sin's story, the story Ryan Malone had allowed her to find in two weeks. Why else would one of the ex-strippers have a yearbook with Sin's picture and name? Then the picture of Sin opening his restaurant arrived on schedule to give the final proof. Once Lord Sin was permanently retired, Ryan Malone was free to live the life he'd built for himself—the lie he'd created.

He'd only made one mistake. He couldn't resist naming his hospital wing for his mother. To do that he had to use her real name, Helen Ivy Malone. He'd found a way to make her life count for something, and it would have been less than honorable for him to hide that name. The platform had been built to shield the base of the monument. It had just been bad luck that Walt had videotaped the plaque.

Sunny had refused to allow herself to believe they had something special, but when he kept after her, touching her, making love to her, protecting her, she'd fallen in love. And all along, he'd been doing whatever he needed to do to manipulate her just as her father's boss had done to him, just as her editor in Martinsville had done to her. And she'd thought she was in charge of her own destiny. Pain cut through her like a shard of ice.

Well, Ryan Malone was wrong. He didn't know Sara Frances Clary. But he was about to. When she was done, the good news would be bad.

She finished the hospital dedication story and started composing the new one, the unmasking of Lord Sin. WTRU would break the hottest local story since they announced that Atlanta had been awarded the 1996 Summer Olympics.

Later, when Ted read the story, he swore. "This is hard to believe. Malone is—well—he's important to Atlanta. And you're the Good-News Girl. Are you sure about this?"

"It's the truth. And we run the truth, don't we?"

Ted let out a deep breath and nodded. "I don't always like it, but WTRU tells the truth. Still, we can't run it without allowing him to give his side."

"I know. You wanted an interview—I guess this is it. It just isn't what I thought it would be. I'll go talk to—Lord Sin."

RYAN SMILED when he opened the door. "I was headed for your place," he said, then pulled her inside and kissed her.

When she didn't respond, he pulled back and frowned.

"What's wrong? Was I too sentimental? Did I sound like a sap when I was talking about the hospital wing and my mother?"

She shook her head. Even now, he kept up the pretense. "You never sound like anything but what you intend, Malone. Why'd you do it? You could have lied to the world but you didn't have to lie to me. Lord Sin wasn't what I expected, but I wouldn't have cared who you were."

She could see the questions dim the welcome in his eyes. "What do you mean, Sunny?"

"Edward Hinton found the yearbook, just as you planned. Lottie verified that Jack Ivy was Lord Sin. Then, just to make sure I had all the proof I needed, you arranged for a photo showing Jack's attendance at the opening of his new restaurant on the Riviera. How did you do that, Ryan? Or do I call you Jack? Or Sin?"

He let his hands drop from her shoulders and turned away. "I'm Ryan Malone. And I'm Lord Sin and I'm Jack. I'm all three."

She followed him, her steps as slow as a death march.

"Jack actually does own Ivy's. I went there for its opening, or rather Jack did. A nice touch, I thought."

"Oh, it was. And I fell for it. Just like I fell for you—even after all that business about trust and commitment. I was perfect, wasn't I. You knew what happened to me in Martinsville. You knew I was ambitious and would do anything to establish my credibility, didn't you?"

"Yes, I knew. But not in the beginning."

"Why, just tell me why you did it?"

"Originally I concealed my identity because I was too young to dance in a place that served alcohol. Then later, Lottie helped Jack Ivy become Lord Sin so that I could earn a living. Finally, I reached a point where I needed to separate the man I was going to become from my past."

"Jackson Lewis Ivy was never a blue-eyed blond, was he?"

"No, the picture in the yearbook was doctored. It was a setup, to convince you that Lord Sin was Jack Ivy who was as different from me as night from day. How'd you figure it out?"

"I might not have, if Walt hadn't videotaped the plaque on your mother's monument, Helen Ivy Malone. You thought that I wouldn't see it."

"Yes. I could have left the Ivy off but that really was her name and my father and his family dishonored her enough when she was alive. I couldn't do that to her in death. I had them build the platform directly in front so that you wouldn't see the base. I knew you would have no reason to come back again later. The cover was to have been left there until the following day. I guess someone moved it."

"But you were Jackson Lewis Ivy. Why not Jackson Lewis Malone?"

"When my mother was admitted to the hospital she told them her name was Helen Ivy. She was afraid my father's family might try to take me. She didn't know what a foolish idea that was. As for my name, I guess she wanted to punish him the only way she could. So I became Jackson for my father and Lewis to connect me forever to the wealth of the Lewis name but I was her son and she was Helen Ivy Malone."

"Or," Sunny said, before she knew she was going to speak, "she named you for Jackson because she still loved him."

"Sentiment and a nickel won't even buy you a cup of coffee, Sunny Clary. You want the truth, haven't you learned that yet?"

"I'm learning that truth means different things to different people."

"So? What are you going to do with this truth?"

She handed him a copy of her story. "That's why I'm here, Ryan. I'm a reporter. I've written the story and I came to give you a chance to respond." She walked back and leaned against the door, willing herself to remain robotlike, lifeless.

If he so much as blinked she'd pick up one of his cream- and-navy-blue decorations and hit him where it hurt the most.

He read, allowing no emotion on his face. Finally, he looked up. "It doesn't matter, Sunny. Not anymore. I always trained myself to be self-sufficient, not to need anybody. And then I met you and you made me think I might be wrong. I was going to tell you, later. But that doesn't matter now." He opened the door and handed the papers back to her. "So you go ahead and run your story. You need credibility. I don't."

SHE HELD the story for three days, telling Ted she was working on Ryan's response. The truth was, she was waiting for Ryan to call her. When he didn't, she turned the story in. The exposé headlined the six o'clock news. The station switchboard lit up like Rockefeller Center at Christmas. Half the callers were outraged that they'd been fooled, the other half furious that Sunny had felled a local icon, some even suggesting that she'd used him to get a story. Sunny didn't answer her phone, not even when an angry Edward Hinton called. He'd been offered a job by one of the rival stations but he didn't like being made to look like a fool. Why hadn't she told him what she found out? The unmasking of Lord Sin was his story, too, and she hadn't bothered to call.

Sunny didn't answer her phone at home either. By midnight her answering machine tape was full of calls from Lottie, Isabella and, finally, her father.

"Sara Frances Clary," his voice said quietly, "I'm surprised at you, ruining a man's good name just to make yourself some kind of front-page news. If this is what your investigative reporting does, I liked the Good-News Girl better. Ryan may have made a mistake but you should have given him a chance to explain."

"I did," she whispered to herself. "He didn't care. He told

me to go ahead and run the story. He's a cold, self-sufficient man who doesn't need anybody, certainly not me."

"That's all I wanted to say," her father continued, "except this. I'm going to ask Lottie to marry me. Don't know whether or not she'll accept, but I'm hoping that she won't hold what you did against me."

Finally, the phone stopped ringing. And the world went silent.

THREE DAYS LATER, after being slapped with a wall of ice by the mayor and his council, she knew she'd made a mistake. City hall might be her beat, but her credibility was lower than ever. So be it, she'd picked herself up before, she'd do it again. Except she seemed to have lost her zeal. At the oddest times she remembered Isabella's birthday and how Ryan danced with the grand old lady, the mayor's awards dinner and Octavius, the boy who singlehandedly cleared a corner lot for a playground, furnished by Ryan. And there was Callie, the child he'd handled so tenderly at the dedication.

The Atlanta community seemed to be even more fascinated and in awe of Ryan Malone. Every morning the news staff handed out stories of events in which he was taking part. But Sunny got none of them. Instead, she covered the kind of crime and corruption that existed in every big city and her stories got lost in the dearth of bad news.

Winter left, pushed aside by a spring as beautiful as winter had been dreary. The azaleas burst into full bloom. Tulips and pansies made masses of color in the flower beds and white dogwood petals fell like errant snowflakes on lawns turning green. Everything was thriving, blossoming, except Sunny. Walt had been reassigned to sports. The good news seemed to be gone and Sunny had never felt so alone.

Bitterness turned her insides into hollow shells of loneliness. She missed Ryan Malone. He'd chased her with a single-mindedness that still astounded her. And she'd destroyed him. Now, when she wanted so badly to hear his voice, he didn't call. She missed Lottie and her father. Another week went by before Isabella finally got through Sunny's wall of silence with her words, "Sunny Clary, you pick up this phone or I'm going to hire all these sunshine boys here at the home to load me up and bring me to your house."

There was no doubt in Sunny's mind that she'd do it. She picked up. "Hello, Isabella. How are you?"

"Better than you, I hope. Not often I'm so wrong about somebody. I thought you and Ryan were right for each other. Then you stick a knife in both your hearts."

"Isabella, my story may be a little ripple in Ryan's stream but he's too big and too important for this to hurt him."

"Hurt? Listen here, girl, you don't know what hurt is—yet. You and Ryan have shoved Humpty Dumpty off the wall. Now get yourself over here. Lottie and I have an idea."

Before Sunny could respond, a dial tone sounded in her ear. If she hadn't already felt bad enough, Isabella's call had pretty much finished any possibility of relieving herself of blame for an unwise decision. And she knew now that she had made a bad choice. No matter what she said or how much she explained, she'd catapulted to success by doing a hatchet job on a man who didn't deserve it. And it had nothing to do with her job. She'd been a fool, thinking that he cared about her. The story had been her revenge. Except the revenge had hit her just as hard.

She'd never considered that what might happen would hurt her heart more than her career.

The final pain was delivered an hour later by special messenger, a manila envelope with a note clipped to several glossy photographs, several negatives and a small box. She was holding the pictures of her and Ryan in the woods. One was a clear shot of his hand in her bra and beneath the curve of her breast. Had she not known about the bee, she would never have believed that he was on a mission of mercy. If these photographs had been merely interesting before, they would be sensational now—in the wake of her story about Lord Sin. But it no longer mattered.

Here they are. Thanks for the help. The new job is going fine. Have to admit I was tempted. Guess Malone knew that, too. I tried to refuse the money. But he did insist on buying them. He said I owed it to you and so did he. *Edward.*

Inside the small box, nestled in fluffy white cotton, was the dead bee. Ryan had saved the thing and bought the photos, too. The printing of the photos would only have made *her* look bad by confirming that she was the kind of hard-nosed reporter who'd do anything to get a story. Suddenly, everything had been reversed. Instead of the Good-News Girl exposing Lord Sin, she'd become the Sinner.

And there was no way she could go back and do it over. What could she have done differently and still stayed true to her vow to tell the truth? That question was harder to answer. She could have put a different slant on the story. Instead of presenting the information as some kind of exposé, she could have portrayed Ryan as the boy who made good.

Her father was right. Isabella was right. She'd made a mistake and she needed to apologize. When she told Ted she needed Walt for her interview with Ryan Malone, he looked puzzled, but he agreed. When Walt found out they were returning to Rainbow House, he didn't even grumble. An hour later, the camera was videotaping the new swimming pool at the retirement center.

"Many of you remember my last story about Ryan Malone, when I revealed his secret past as the infamous Lord Sin. Today, the Good-News Girl wants to talk about a hero. My story about Lord Sin was the truth but the bad news is that it hurt someone who never did anything but good. Ryan Malone's life was one of protecting those he cared about, those who preferred not to have their misfortune spread across the news and those who never knew where their help came from. And I made him sound like a fraud.

"I made a mistake," Sunny admitted. "Not in reporting the truth. I had to do that, but in telling the story of Lord Sin in anger. I thought the only reason he was interested in me was because he wanted me to help him make Lord Sin disappear. I let that color my judgment. When I told his story, I did it to make myself look good. Now I want Atlanta to care about a man with a good heart as much as I do. A hero who not only builds swimming pools to help those with arthritis exercise their limbs, but sends a bus to pick up those who don't live in Rainbow House. I want all of you to know that what's in the heart is the important thing, not what those of us in the media report.

"So, if you're listening, Ryan, thank you from all of us. What Atlanta needs is more good news and—" she gave a wicked smile "—more satin sheets. This is Sunny Clary reporting from Rainbow House."

When the camera lights went off, Isabella clapped. "Very nice, Sunny. But you were too hard on yourself. In the beginning, Ryan did set out to use you. That changed. For the first time, Ryan fell in love, but he didn't know how to tell you. Lord Sin was a stripper and unless you've been a stripper you can't know what the world thinks about that profession. He was scared he'd lose you and he thought that once Lord Sin was gone, his past would be gone, too."

"Did you know he bought those pictures, the ones of the bee in my bra, to protect me? Why did he do that?"

"Ryan has always looked out for those he cares about."

An hour later, Sunny was still sitting on Isabella's couch. She dropped her head and let out a deep sigh. "What am I going to do?"

"I wonder if Ryan will see your story," Isabella said.

"Why wouldn't he see it?" Lottie asked, turning on the television. "What time will it be on?"

Sunny glanced at her watch. "If they run it on the hour, it ought to be now."

At that moment a shot of Rainbow House came on the screen. Lottie picked up the phone, put it on speaker, and punched in the number. The answering machine came on. "Ryan, if you're there—"

"I am, Lottie. What do you want?"

"Turn on WTRU."

"Why? Is Sunny exposing a little old grandfather who mugs pigeons?"

Then he hushed as Sunny's voice came over the speaker, repeating her story about a man who should be a hero. When she signed off, there was a long silence, followed by a click and a dial tone.

"He doesn't believe me. I've ruined everything, haven't I?" Sunny asked. "What am I going to do?"

"What do you want to do?" the old woman asked.

"Somehow, I have to let him know that I don't care if he was a stripper. I'll take up stripping myself, if that's what it takes."

"That's it!"Lottie shouted. "That's what you'll do. I'll teach you a routine. Tonight, the Good-Time Girl will strip for Lord Sin."

SUNNY LOOKED AT HERSELF in the mirror and cringed. Her nipples were covered with red roses. The G-string was green and sewn with fake leaves. The rest of her was embarrassingly bare. "Lottie, I'll never be able to go through with this."

"Sure you will. You've got the moves down fine. We just have to get you covered up." Lottie held out a shimmering see-through halter. "Put this on first." She looped the ties at the back around Sunny's neck and handed them to her.

With a groan, Sunny tied the straps under her chin giving herself a sparkling bow tie. "Look at me. I'm all hair and legs. He'll laugh me right out of his apartment."

"Just so long as you take him with you," Lottie said. "I think it's time that Lord Sin had a dose of his own medicine."

Sunny struggled to get the halter on and looked into the mirror. When she saw how skimpy her clothes were, she shook her head. "Why wear anything at all?"

"So you'll have something to take off. Trust me, Sunny. This is just what Ryan needs to make him see the truth. He's been harder on himself than the public ever thought about being. He's gone into hiding, neglecting his office, his friends, everything. But it isn't the story that did it, it's losing you."

"Maybe, but this is a bad idea, Lottie. I'll have to come up with something more spectacular than this to convince him I've changed."

"Yeah," Lottie said with a grin. "First you have to get his attention. Talk dirty."

Half an hour later, Sunny had added a short skirt, a jacket which hugged the bow from her halter and buttoned down the front and a pair of shoes with three-inch heels. "Okay, you taught me the moves. How do I manage the dirty talk?"

Lottie handed Sunny the tape recorder, already loaded with the music they'd rehearsed. "That part of the seduction is up to you. You'll think of something."

Sunny carried Lottie's recorder and a single red rose, apprehension growing by the mile as she drove herself to

Ryan's building. The pasties abraded her nipples with every move she made. That, combined with the thought of what she was about to do, drew her nerves into a tight wire of tension. She was beginning to appreciate what a stripper endured.

At the Malone Building, Sunny shrugged off the valet parking attendant with a shake of her head and drove her Cutlass beneath the building to the darkest corner of the top parking deck. She pulled the ties of her raincoat tighter, gathered up her recorder and the rose and started into the building, feeling as if she was stuffed.

"Evening, Ms. Clary," the guard in the lobby said. "Shall I let Mr. Malone know you're here?"

"No. Please don't. I want to surprise him." Surprise? That was likely to be an understatement. This was going to be a disaster. Twice, she almost changed her mind and returned to the lobby. At Ryan's door she folded the tape recorder under her arm, took a deep breath and rang the bell.

Inside the penthouse Ryan was talking to the guard. "Are you sure?"

"Of course. I know Ms. Clary. She's dressed a little odd but it's her."

The bell rang once, then repeatedly. An unexpected, forbidden tremor rippled down his backbone. He didn't know why she was here and he didn't want to feel—not anything, certainly not anticipation. Then his hand was on the door and it was open.

But there was no one there.

Only the sound of tom-toms.

Then a leg curled around the doorframe, followed by one arm and a hand holding a long-stemmed red rose.

"What the hell?"

The crash of cymbals brought into view both legs and a sexy little business suit. The door closed. She placed the tape recorder on the floor and bent her head forward. He couldn't see her face, only a mass of unruly hair hanging in a fall of red. She merely stood, her hands resting on her thighs. Then, as the music changed, his visitor began to circle her hips. She lifted her head and moved forward until her palms were pressing his chest. Then she gave a shake to her head and pushed him away. Every move in time with the music, she turned her back, unbuttoned and dropped her jacket. She leaned forward and looked at him between her legs, the rose clasped in her teeth.

Ryan lost every smidgen of air he'd ever drawn in.

"You didn't come to me, Sin," she whispered. "I waited. But my bed grows cold in the darkness. You made me yours. You promised me a lover, but you didn't come. Now I've come to you. I'm real, my darling, and I'm filled with love for you."

She stood, unfastened a snap at her waist and dropped the short skirt, revealing her bare bottom before she turned to face him again. "What's the matter, Sin?" she said, and ripped away the top leaf from her G-string. "Am I getting to you? Do you want to touch me? I want to touch you." She jerked off another leaf. "I want to spend the rest of my life touching you." With her hands she simulated the same motions he'd made on stage, the seduction of the imaginary lover. Sunny did things with the rose she carried that Sin had never imagined. He was ready to explode.

"Why?" he asked, his voice so tight that he could hardly speak.

"Because I love you, the man you were and the man you are." She untied the bow that held the see-through halter around her neck. The halter was gone. And all he could see were the rosettes she wore on her nipples. "Tell me that you love me." She plucked the final leaf. "Lord Sin," she said with a purr in her voice, "your lady of the green fire has come to you."

She was magnificent, a golden-skinned woman wearing nothing but two rosettes, a woman as wicked as sin. And Ryan knew they were a perfect match. He smiled and approached her, pulling his shirt over his head and unbuttoning his pants. "Who taught you my moves?" he whispered.

"You did."

Moments later he stood facing her, wearing nothing but an erection and a smile. "You learn well. But to create a world of fantasy is temporary. To make it real, you have to go there with me. Will you?"

She gave him a long, heated look and said, "Take me."

He did.

At midnight he slid from the bed and disappeared, reappearing moments later with champagne, chocolates and strawberries, which he spread across the satin sheets.

Sunny caught the chocolate as it slid toward the edge.

"We're going to have to do something about these sheets, Ryan," she said.

"Now that I've made love to you here, we will," he said, sitting cross-legged across the bottom of the bed and opening the champagne. "I've ordered burgundy knit bed linens. I want you to have what makes you happy."

She took two berries, put one in her mouth and bit into it, the juice beading on her tongue before she said, "Then you aren't throwing me out?"

He filled the fluted glass, took a sip and handed it to her. "I'm locking the door and throwing away the key. I love you, Sunny. I want to marry you."

She dropped the second berry and watched wide-eyed as it slid down her chest and disappeared into the covers. "Marry you? Oh, Ryan. I don't know. I never expected that."

"I never expected to ask a woman either. But I'm asking

you, Sara Frances Clary. Be my wife. Separate, we're alone. Together, we're complete.''

"Are you sure you want a wife? A wife is forever."

"I'm sure."

"I'm sorry I told the world your secret."

"I'm glad you did. Now Jack Ivy doesn't have to live on the Riviera. No more secrets, Sunny."

"Are you sure, Ryan? I know now I want to have a family, children. But I still want to report the good news. Will you mind?"

"I'll buy you a television station if that's what you want."

She lifted her face in question. "Are you that rich?"

"No, but Lord Sin will come out of retirement to dance again if we need him."

She smiled. "I'll always need him. I love Lord Sin. I love Ryan Malone and I love Jack Ivy for creating both of them. So, if you want me, the answer is yes. Just promise me that the only woman Lord Sin ever dances for is me."

She leaned back, her red hair a slash of color on his white satin sheets.

"I do," he whispered and kissed her.

_____ Epilogue _____

EASTER CAME EARLY that year and on the Tuesday evening after, Lottie and Reverend Clary stepped into the penthouse apartment, beaming like two kids who'd found the prize in the egg hunt.

"Lottie Lamour! What have you been up to?" Ryan demanded. He was standing behind Sunny, both arms possessively around her waist.

"Lottie Clary!" Byron corrected, pulling Lottie close and giving her a goofy kiss. "Daughter, be polite. Say good morning to your stepmother."

"Pop, don't be silly, I don't have a stepmother."

"You do now."

Sunny looked at Ryan who was looking at Lottie who was practically devouring Byron Clary with her eyes. "We got married last night," Lottie said. "Of course it was a justice of the peace but it was legal. When we get back to St. Mary's we're going to have a church wedding. I'm going to wear a white dress. Of course—" she blushed "—I ought not, but Byron said I should."

Sunny pulled Ryan into the living room before he played the outraged father and paddled Lottie. "Come in and tell us about it." She sat down on the couch. "You actually got married? "

Byron nodded. "There are still places where you can get a blood test, license and get married, all in one place. I mean we didn't want to...wait. We just stopped by on the way to

Lottie's to tell you so you wouldn't worry if you discovered my car outside of her place all night."

Sunny started to laugh. Her daddy hadn't said a word about the fact that she'd moved into Ryan Malone's apartment before they were married but he was worried about what she might think of him if he spent the night at Lottie's. "You're really married? You eloped?"

"Yes, we are," he answered, coming toward her. "We did. I know it must be a shock. It was a shock to me. I think I fell in love with her the first moment I saw her."

"Please, don't be angry," Lottie said. "But I knew I couldn't let him go back to South Georgia without me. And he's a minister. I've never been a bride before, Ryan, and Byron wanted me to be his wife before we— No, I'm not going to apologize. I love him and I married him. It's just too bad two other people I know haven't done the same thing."

Sunny planted a stern expression on her face and stood. "Sit down, Pop. There's something I want you to hear. Ryan, please turn on the television to WTRU news."

Moments later Sunny's smiling face flashed across the screen. "Good evening, Atlanta, this is Sunny Clary, with more good news. At least the news is good for me. For all you Lord Sin fans, I'm afraid the news is bad. Several months ago, on his retirement, I revealed the truth about the identity of the most famous entertainer in Atlanta's history and the hero he'd become as his alter ego. Now I have an exclusive on his next endeavor."

She held up her left hand so that the light could catch the facets of the diamond ring on her finger. If anybody in the viewing audience thought the engagement ring looked remotely like a honeybee, it was never reported.

"Two weeks from today," Sunny said, "WTRU will be covering the wedding of Sara Frances Clary and the former Lord Sin, Ryan Malone."

The tape faded to black and the next shot was of Sunny *and* Ryan. Ryan smiled at the television audience. "The bad news in this story is that the honeymoon is private."

The kiss that followed wasn't.

Later, the WTRU weatherman struggled to make sense of the sudden increase in the Atlanta temperature. Sunny could have told him it wasn't sunspots. The jump came from the exhaling of the television audience and the chorus of "Ahhhs" that swept across the city. She could have told them to be prepared for the same phenomenon in about eight months—but for now, she'd save that "good news."

Come escape with Harlequin's new

Series Sampler

Four great full-length Harlequin novels bound together in one fabulous volume and at an unbelievable price.

Be transported back in time with a Harlequin Historical® novel, get caught up in a mystery with Intrigue®, be tempted by a hot, sizzling romance with Harlequin Temptation®, or just enjoy a down-home all-American read with American Romance®.

You won't be able to put this collection down!

On sale February 2000 at your favorite retail outlet.